# Tommy Mac

# Tommy Mac

## Margaret Stuart Barry

### Illustrated by Dinah Dryhurst

Kestrel Books

KESTREL BOOKS
Penguin Books Ltd,
Harmondsworth, Middlesex, England

Text Copyright © 1972 by Margaret Stuart Barry
Illustrations Copyright © 1972 by Longman Young Books

First published 1972
under the Longman Young Books Imprint
Reprinted 1974, 1977, 1981 and 1984

ISBN 0 7226 5053 1

Printed in Hong Kong by
Hing Yip Printing Co.

# Contents

# Contents

# 1. Unwelcome Help

Tommy Mac sat on the doorstep of Number Seven, Paradise Way, and surveyed the morning scene through sheets of yellowish rain. There was a brewery further down the hill which constantly blew out black smoke, and the rain was stopping the smoke from rising and was sending it up the street instead. This never failed to madden Mrs Mac, but this particular morning it didn't—she was in bed with 'flu and too ill to notice.

It was rare for Mrs Mac to take to her bed, but Dr Azanti had called the night before and told her that she must. When she had protested he suggested she ask a relation to come and help with the children, and so Aunt Lil was coming to stay.

'And at half term!' moaned Tommy. 'Do we *have* to have Aunt Lil, Dad?'

'Yes lad, we do.' Mr Mac sounded stern.

'Couldn't our Maureen do us?' Tommy persisted.

After all, Maureen was almost fifteen and nearly ready to leave school. She was always talking about getting married, and carrying on as if she were already grown-up.

'Maureen'd do us right enough!' laughed Mr Mac. 'We'd *all* be in our beds if she took over!'

Tommy agreed. Maureen was interested in little else other than her own face and the problem of how to disguise it behind bucketsful of lardy eyeshadow. Tommy knew, too, that his dad must carry on his job as a long-distance lorry driver if they were to eat and stay away from the 'Nashy'. Aunt Lil seemed to be the only answer.

Mr Mac cuffed his son round the ear. 'Nothing lasts forever,' he grinned.

Aunt Lil was always going on about 'wasting not' and 'wanting not' yet she arrived in a taxi. Something had happened to her knee, she explained. The Macs nudged each other. There was always something the matter with Aunt Lil. They had taken bets as to which part of her anatomy would be affected this time but, for once, none of them had won.

Aunt Lil needed immediate refreshment. She had had 'such a ghastly journey' and the porters had been 'so unhelpful'. She had come all the way from London, Clapham to be exact, and was really rather posh in comparison with the Mac family.

'Hi really ham most hawfully tired,' she said to Mr Mac. 'But of course when hi 'eard Marge was hill hi came at once.' Aunt Lil threw her aitches with practised ease from one word to another.

Mr Mac shuffled. He glanced uncomfortably down. Aunt Lil's fat legs plummeted down to the tiniest of pointed shoes. He was glad Mrs Mac wasn't that smart.

Aunt Lil finished her tea and then heaved herself up the stairs to see Mrs Mac. As soon as she had disappeared, Charlie began to howl. Charlie Mac was only four and he wanted his mam back downstairs. He felt that Aunt Lil—that woman who had just finished off all the ham—wasn't going to see to him the way Mrs Mac did. Mags and Kate, no more than a couple of years older, felt it too.

Tommy rinsed his own cup and escaped into the welcome rain. It was washing the streets and carrying last night's chip papers past the blocked grids towards the dock road. Tommy selected a particularly greasy piece of paper and raced it to the end of Paradise Way. It had never occurred to him that the name 'Paradise' did not exactly suit the grimy, unbeautiful street in which he had been born. He had once heard his grandfather comment, 'When I die, I hope to find heaven like Paradise Way, with its cats, and old women in shawls, and the kiddies playing hopscotch down the hill.' Grandad had then suddenly 'passed on', and Tommy often wondered if he were still around; perhaps in the warehouse he was now passing, or maybe in the cellar of Stevey's favourite ale house. Stevey was Tommy Mac's elder brother and he worked on the docks when the fancy took him. Was Grandad perhaps under the 'bomby', pushing up the green dock leaves?

Tommy arrived at Michael O'Rafferty's house. Raff was a member of his gang. Rocky Chai was also at home, and the three boys went down to the river. They weren't a big gang but they were nevertheless respected in the neighbourhood.

'We've got our Aunt Lil stoppin' with us,' Tommy announced at once.

'Is that bad?' Raff wanted to know.

'Of course it's bad!' scolded Tommy. 'She's an old witch.' He had heard his father saying that once.

'Yes, but she's doin' for you, in't she?' said Chai reasonably.

Tommy Mac didn't want to be reasonable. He liked the feeling of being able to go home at any odd hour of the day and find his mother always there; always scrubbing the steps and the pavement beyond; always peeling potatoes and washing dishes; always picking up toys and folding newspapers; always carrying Stevey's empty beer bottles into the back kitchen. Aunt Lil, on the other hand, seemed to require all sorts of extra help.

'Course it's bad,' said Tommy again.

The boys watched an oil tanker for ten minutes or so in complete silence, then Chai said, 'But she's not dying though, is she?'

'Who?'

'Your Mam.'

'Course not!' cried Tommy.

'Well, what I mean is,' went on Chai, nervously, 'yer Aunt Lil won't be staying forever.'

Tommy knew what Chai meant. But he was in a bad mood, the sort of mood which takes a long and miserable time to wear off. He trudged home sulking.

There was no welcoming smell of cooking as Tommy entered the house. That, for a start, wasn't normal. Stevey had actually gone down to Alexander dock to do a bit of graft—work, that is. He had been going to get lardied up and take out a girl, which was his hobby, but with Aunt Lil in the way he couldn't dress up properly. Charlie was sitting on the kitchen floor playing bowls with a bag of potatoes. Mags and Kate had disappeared to the play centre. And Aunt Lil was seated in the parlour doing nothing better than reading the paper. Tommy Mac was shocked. Nobody sat in the parlour as a rule, except at Christmas and times like that. It was kept polished and tidy, the plastic sweet-peas were rinsed in soapy water now and then, and the curtains kept part closed— just the same as all the front curtains were drawn down the rest of the street. Aunt Lil's head darted backwards and forwards as she read. She didn't even notice Tommy. Disgusted, he crept upstairs to see his mother.

Mrs Mac was propped up against a mountain of pillows and cushions. Her plump face was red and very shiny. She looked ill. But at the sight of Tommy she said, 'Aah! Come here love. How are you?'

'There's no tea yet, Mam,' said Tommy, sitting on the bed. He ruffled his thick hair and scowled. He knew that in a short while his father would be home with the lorry and he was usually ready to eat a horse—providing it was well cooked, of course.

'Don't worry, lad,' wheezed Mrs Mac, 'our Lil'l look after you.'

Tommy rubbed his nose energetically on his sleeve. 'Aunt Lil is . . .' he began indignantly. But he did not finish; his mother was gasping and pulling at the buttons of her cardigan.

'Is Charlie alright?' she panted.

Charlie! Tommy tore downstairs to look for him. He could have been absolutely anywhere, but he was still sitting on the kitchen floor. He had grown tired of playing bowls with the potatoes and had decided to make them into chips. The knife drawer was too high for him to reach but he had found a set of Stevey's tools, and he now had a hammer and a chisel, two screwdrivers and a sharp saw. The chips were all different sizes but Charlie was pleased with them. He was pretending to be Ma McCann, who owned the fish and chip shop in Paradise Way. He had also found Maureen's new copy of *Real Love*, had torn it into pieces, and was using it to wrap up his chips. For once Tommy was not amused. He grabbed Charlie and whisked him upstairs.

'Little love!' cried Mrs Mac when she saw him. She pulled off his shoes and he snuggled down next to her. Charlie sucked his thumb and settled blissfully against his mother's comfortable chest.

'You'd better go and give your aunt a hand,' suggested Mrs Mac. 'I expect she's rushed off her feet.'

Still upset at the sight of his mother laid up— she was like a great whale stranded on a beach— Tommy went downstairs.

At the last minute, Aunt Lil hurried into the kitchen. Unable to find any potatoes, she dodged out to the corner shop and returned with hot pies and peas. The family munched in silence. Mr Mac, who had been driving for ten hours, slipped away to the nearest Chinese restaurant to fill up, and the children retired, unwashed, to bed.

Tommy Mac was not easily beaten. Next day, with Raff and Chai to help him, he set about making plans.

'She's getting no better,' he said.

'Your Mam do you mean?'

'No, stupid. Aunt Lil.'

'But she's helping you.'

'She's not,' snapped Tommy. 'She's in the way. I could help better'n what she does.'

'D'you want her to go then?' asked Chai unnecessarily.

'Yes,' said Tommy.

And from then on the plan became clear.

'D'you know what, Aunt Lil,' said Tommy later.

Aunt Lil didn't.

'Me and my gang thought it would be a good idea if we helped you with the house and all the extra work and all that.'

Aunt Lil rubbed her sore knee. She had been thinking secretly that Tommy was the difficult one of the family. Perhaps she had been mistaken. Innocently, she handed him a shopping list.

Tommy, Raff and Chai set out for the shops. Later they stood at the kitchen sink peeling potatoes and scraping carrots.

'Hi can't get used to that old stove,' Aunt Lil was complaining. 'Hat 'ome I've got an oven with a glass door. My Albert says there's no one cooks like me.'

The gang could well believe it but said nothing. Aunt Lil felt that the meal was well under way and put on her hat and went off to look at the shops in the city. She would get back just before Mr Mac came in and dish up.

As soon as she was gone, Tommy and his gang put on the toaster and the egg pan and they made Mrs Mac a nice poached egg. *She* mustn't suffer, whatever happened. Then they set the table. They put on the potatoes and the carrots and, when they were almost done, Aunt Lil returned with a satisfied smile and a new hat.

In dribs and drabs the others turned up. Mr

Mac was hungry as usual. Mags and Kate fought to sit next to him, and Maureen filed her nails over her empty plate and waited for someone to put something on it.

Beaming with efficiency, Aunt Lil sailed across the kitchen to the stove. She shook the potatoes and carrots busily into their dishes. Then she opened the oven door. The oven was cold. It was also empty.

'Where's the mince?' gasped Aunt Lil. 'Where's the mince?'

'Mince?' asked Tommy. 'What mince?'

'The mince you . . . I cooked.'

'I didn't know there was mince,' said Tommy. His eyes grew rounder and rounder.

'Did you know about mince?' he asked Raff and Chai who were still standing there.

'No, didn't know about no mince,' they lied joyfully.

'But it was on the shopping list!' Aunt Lil was becoming hysterical and growing redder by the minute.

'Didn't see it,' said Tommy.

'Mustn't have noticed it,' Chai lied expertly. 'We thought we'd just help, doin' the potatoes and things.'

'Thought *you* was doing the dinner. We was just trying to help,' added Raff.

They had rehearsed this speech all morning. It was going very nicely. Then Chai remembered his most important line: 'We thought when you were in town all day, all them hours, *you* were buying the meat.' He had never looked so innocent in his life. Tommy glanced at him admiringly. Aunt Lil opened and shut her mouth like an outsize carp.

There was a thump, thump on the stairs. It was Charlie coming down on his bottom. He was wearing his tee-shirt on his head like a pirate's cap and he had both socks tied under his chin to look like a beard.

'Mam says she wants din din.'

He pushed the cat off his mother's chair because it was going to be his ship—the chair, that is.

'Lil,' said Mr Mac. His hands were clenched on the table, white and tight round the knuckles. They looked like a couple of shovels, Tommy thought.

'Weren't *you* supposed to be doing this dinner, Lil?' Mr Mac went on.

'Well, Tommy . . .' Aunt Lil started.

'Tommy is only a lad. We don't usually have him cooking for us.' Mr Mac, usually so kind, sounded very stern.

'Pussy wants his din din,' interrupted Charlie, pushing the cat away with a cushion to stop it from getting back into the 'ship'. 'Aunt Lil, our cat-pussy wants his din.'

Charlie went into a long explanation of how his mother usually gave the cat its dinner; who usually gave all of them their dinners, and that Tommy had never given anybody their dinners because he wasn't old enough.

Fuming, but lost for words, Aunt Lil collected the dishes and clattered them noisily into the sink.

'You were great!' Tommy congratulated his gang later. 'Bet she'll go home now.'

But Aunt Lil would not be moved. She would not speak to Mr Mac, but she made a great show of cooking from then onwards. They had chicken and roast potatoes, grilled steak with mushrooms, sherry trifles, smoked salmon; she spent more housekeeping money in a couple of days than Mrs Mac went through in a month. Stevey and Maureen thought it was great. Even Charlie's cat-pussy was beginning to change it's mind about Aunt Lil. But Tommy could see that his father— and his mother—were getting anxious. He understood, wisely, that Monday was a scouse day, not a chicken day. And that butter was for spreading under jam and not for pouring willy nilly over steak.

Tommy went for a walk, a thing he often did when he was trying to puzzle something out. But, although he trailed round the block three times, he could not come up with a good plan for getting rid of his aunt.

It was then that Charlie solved the problem single-handed, but in a way that not even Tommy would have wished.

Charlie Mac, bored with being left on his own, had been upstairs to see his mother, only to find her asleep. Aunt Lil was out somewhere; shopping for more food, he supposed. The house was quiet and cold and Charlie wandered sadly into the kitchen in search of the warmth of the kitchen fire. But the grate was cold and empty; Aunt Lil hadn't bothered to light a fire that day.

'I know, *I'll* light a fire!' Charlie said to himself. 'I'll light the fire for my Mam.'

He knew where the matches were kept and that the firelighters were kept in the coal scuttle. There were a few lumps of coal in the grate.

Charlie lit a match and threw it on the firelighters. At the same time, Stevey's vest, which was airing on the clothes maiden, fell off. Mysteriously, it caught fire and landed on the hearth rug. Little orange spots spread across the rug like wriggling glow worms. Charlie tried to beat them out with his hands, but they hurt. Smoke started to rise and drift towards the open window.

'Mam!' yelled Charlie.

The back door burst open and Mrs Evans, who lived next door, dashed in. The fire was not a large one and she soon stamped it out, but Charlie's hands were very much the worse for wear.

When he returned from hospital later that day he found that Aunt Lil had gone, his father was home and his mother was back downstairs.

'I've been in a bamulance!' he whooped.

Everyone wanted to make a fuss of Charlie, especially his mother, who was pale but much better. And no one mentioned Aunt Lil again.

## 2. Ma Carney and the Useful Junk

It was a sunny, blowy Saturday afternoon. Sunny, blowy days always made Tommy Mac restless. He either wanted to make something, or he wanted to walk. Today he felt like walking. He rounded up his two friends, Raff and Chai. They were in the same mood.

'Let's go down and see Ma Carney in the market,' Tommy suggested.

'All right,' agreed Raff and Chai together.

'Mam,' yelled Tommy, 'I'm just going down to town for a couple of hours.'

'All right, our lad,' shouted Mrs Mac. 'Mind the traffic.'

It was only two and a half miles to the town. The three boys leaped along the pavements like young animals, enjoying the sunshine and the freedom from school. On Saturdays, they were anything they wanted to be: cowboys, gangsters, detectives, tramps; it was a glorious feeling.

'Isn't it smashing not to be in school!' sang Tommy.

'Oh, I dunno,' said Chai. 'I got a star for my writing on Friday.'

'Oh, goody goody gumdrops,' mocked Tommy.

'Shut up,' snapped Chai. 'You've never had a star for *anything*, have you?'

'No, but I'd rather be outside, finding out things and really living and having adventures.'

'Yes of course,' said Raff, 'but how do you have adventures round here, for instance?'

'You look for 'em, that's how,' said Tommy. 'There are adventures all round. All you have to do is to *look* for them.'

'How?' asked Chai.

'Well, I dunno,' said Tommy irritably. 'One doesn't know when adventures are coming or they wouldn't be adventures, would they?' He considered. 'One just keeps ones eyes and ears open ready.'

When they arrived at the market, the smell of fish greeted them. It was a powerful smell.

'Whew!' gasped Tommy. 'Fancy working down here all day.' He both hated and loved the smell. And after a short time one even got used to it. And after a lot more time one didn't even notice it at all.

'Look at them dogs,' said Tommy.

'*Those* dogs,' corrected Chai.

'No, I mean them; them over there.'

'Those with the patchy eyes?'

'Yes. I wish I had some money.'

'Your Mam wouldn't be very pleased,' commented Raff sensibly. 'There are enough kids in your house already without taking a pup home.'

'My Mam isn't like that,' answered Tommy, scornfully. 'And a dog isn't like having another kid: nappies and bottles and rubbish everywhere.

It'd be out all day in the street like other normal dogs. And Mags, Kate and our Charlie drop enough food on the floor for it to live off. I bet it would be jolly useful—like having a lekky cleaner. Only you wouldn't have to plug it in anywhere or lift it in and out of cupboards.'

Chai and Raff were silent. There seemed no answer to Tommy's argument. They felt that there should have been.

'I like that brown one best,' decided Tommy. 'Hey mister, how much's that brown one?'

'Forty pence,' said the dog-man, 'twenty-five to you.'

'Keep it for me. I'll be back in half an hour.'

'How are you going to afford it, Tommy?' asked Chai. 'You haven't even got two pence for the bus.'

'I'll use my brains, that's how. I'll go round to the back of the fruit market; chop a few orange boxes and sell them as bundles of firewood. People are glad of firewood all chopped ready. I might even make enough money to buy *two* dogs.'

He could see himself setting up as a dog breeder. His eyes gleamed at the thought. People in Paradise Way were fond of dogs. He'd probably make a fortune. And then his mam and all the kids could move out to a better house.

He was thinking of the better house, and had just got as far as designing the swimming pool, when he found himself slap up against Ma Carney's stall. It was half empty.

'Hullo Ma Carney,' he greeted her, surprised.

'Hullo boys,' the old woman answered.

'What's the matter with your stall today?' Tommy Mac asked.

There were a few cups and saucers dotted about here and there; a chipped statue of a sparsely dressed lady being dragged along by a red setter; an Indian shawl, and a small pile of gramophone records.

'Is this all you got then?'

'Yes love, that's all I got today,' sighed Ma

Carney. She pulled her shawl tightly under her chin and looked forlorn.

'But you usually have piles of stuff, Ma,' persisted Tommy.

'Yes, we were looking forward to seeing what you'd got,' added Raff. 'We walked all the way to town just to see what you'd got.'

'And to see you too,' Chai added thoughtfully.

'I know, and I look forward to seeing *you*,' Ma Carney said. 'But you see, boys, I've been ill, and I couldn't get around the 'ouses to get no stuff. I'm thinking of packing the whole job in.'

'You can't do *that!*' gasped Tommy Mac. 'Saturday afternoons would be rotten if you weren't here. It'd be just rotten.'

'That's nice of you, Tommy love, but everyone's got to pack up work sometime. And now seems like a very good time.'

'We won't let you do it,' Tommy exclaimed passionately. 'Give us your cart and *we'll* find you some stuff to sell, won't we boys?'

'Lots of it,' echoed Raff and Chai.

But out of sight, they asked, 'Where?'

'Oh nearby—somewhere. There must be *plenty* of houses with junk in 'em. You know those old houses behind the museum which are getting mollyshized,' continued Tommy.

'Demolished you mean.'

'Well, whatever—they're *big* houses, let's try them first.'

Ma Carney's 'cart' was really an old pram. 'The last time a baby was in this must have been in Queen Victoria's time,' commented Raff, laughing.

'Don't be soft! We could flog it to the museum if it was that old,' scoffed Tommy.

'Hey look!' exclaimed Chai. 'Those houses look likely.'

They knocked on the door of the first. A fat woman in an apron and head scarf opened the door and slammed it again before the boys had even opened their mouths.

'Huh! I wouldn't have anything out of *her* rotten house . . . probably have fleas handed out free with *her* rubbish,' said Chai.

'They'd have jumped off by the time we got back to the market,' said Tommy Mac philosophically. 'You can't afford to be too fussy in this business you know. This is the way millionaires start off. If they'd bothered about a few fleas and things when they was starting off buying and selling things, they wouldn't have got to be millionaires.'

'All right, all right,' snapped Chai. '*You* knock at the next door and *you* push the pram.'

'Windy!' mocked Tommy, running up to the next house and belting on the doorknocker.

This time, he had his mouth open and his foot ready to stick in the door, as he'd seen the rent collector doing in Paradise Way on a Friday. The foot trick wasn't necessary: a bird-like little woman opened the door wide and beamed at them.

'Well, well, well,' she chirped, 'I've got little visitors have I?' She smoothed her shiny black dress. 'Come in, come in.'

'Do you think she's potty?' asked Chai in a low voice.

'Dunno,' said Raff. 'Get in there quick before she changes her mind.'

'Will your nice pram be safe out there, I wonder?' asked the birdy-lady.

'She *is* potty,' whispered Chai again out of the corner of his mouth.

'What did you say?' asked the old lady, spinning round with remarkable speed.

'I said isn't the pottery in your parlour lovely,' stuttered Chai, turning crimson with embarrassment.

'Ah, what a perceptive little fellow you are,' cried the old lady, delighted. 'I can tell you appreciate fine things. Not many do, not many do. Now then boys, what can I do for you?'

Tommy waded in. 'We've got a dear old friend,' he began, filling his lungs for a speech, 'she's got a stall in the market with nothing to sell on it. She's very, very old, and hasn't eaten for three whole weeks—just drinks water all the time. And she's getting thinner and thinner. She's getting so weak—friends have to help her to get her to work—and she's hardly not got any friends left. And now her landlord—who's got *thousands* of houses but wants more and more money—is going to throw her out of her shabby little house if she can't pay the rent tonight. And she can't pay if she hasn't any junk to sell, and she hasn't, so we're trying to collect it for her because she'd probably just die straight away if she was thrown out in the street—and she will be if she can't pay the rent.'

Raff and Chai stared at Tommy Mac in dumb admiration. The birdy-lady blew her nose very hard and cleaned her spectacles on her apron.

'What wonderful friends you must be,' she said, 'and isn't it amazing, just amazing that you should call at my house! Follow me and you'll see why I say that.'

She led the way to the top of the house and flung open a door. 'There!' she cried. 'All yours, for that poor old lady, that dear distressed soul.'

The three boys stared, astonished. The room was choc-a-bloc with junk.

'Good junk,' whistled Tommy Mac softly. 'Can we have all this?'

'Certainly you can,' chuckled the old lady. 'I've been trying to get rid of this for nearly ten whole years. It used to belong to an old gentleman who lived here as a lodger. He disappeared one day, and he didn't leave his rent either. Never mind, he was a nice old soul really. I expect he's long since dead. I've asked the corporation to move this until I'm blue in the face. Now it's yours.'

'Thanks a lot, Mrs . . .?'

'Finch,' said the old lady.

'There's a bird called a finch,' giggled Chai, as they were carrying the junk down the ricketty old stairs.

'Shut up,' hissed Tommy. 'She's a jolly decent old bird. Ma Carney won't get thrown out in the street now, thanks to her.'

'I didn't know she was really going to be thrown out,' said Chai.

'No, well get a move on anyway . . .'

Soon the pram was full to overflowing. They secured the heap of junk with an old clothes line, thanked Mrs Finch once again, and charged down the street to the market place.

'Lor' love us!' exclaimed Ma Carney when she saw them coming. 'You didn't knock it off, did you?' she asked suspiciously.

'No,' panted Raff, 'this nice old woman gave it to us. We didn't pinch it.'

'S'truth,' Tommy assured her.

'Well, I haven't seen stuff like this for *years*,'

said Ma Carney happily. 'Help me set it out, loves.'

People began to saunter across to the stall, and soon money clinked into Ma Carney's apron pocket.

'What about your pup, Tommy?' asked Raff.

'Oh gosh! I'd forgotten about that. It's too late now. I'll get one next Saturday—only it won't be the same dog,' he said regretfully. Suddenly he wanted that brown pup more than anything else in the world.

A large important-looking man was talking to Ma Carney. Tommy Mac wandered over to listen.

'Yes, it's rather a pleasant looking picture,' the man was saying. 'How much are you asking for it madam?' he asked, in a not-really-interested-sort-of-voice.

But Ma Carney was used to guessing when a customer really wanted something, and she knew that the important-looking gentleman wanted her picture.

'Fifty pounds,' she said.

'No, no,' said the man. 'Thirty pounds, no more.

'Forty-five pounds,' said Ma Carney, pink with excitement.

'Forty pounds,' said the important-looking man.

'No, forty-five pounds I said, and forty-five pounds I'll get for it.' Ma Carney was very firm and wouldn't be budged from her price.

'Very well,' the important-looking man agreed suddenly. He paid for the picture and carried it off under his arm, very pleased with himself.

'Wow!' exclaimed Tommy, Raff and Chai together. 'Fancy that mouldy old picture being worth forty-five pounds.'

'It was probably worth a lot more,' said Ma Carney, 'but I'm satisfied. You've brought me a lot of luck today. Now I'll be able to do what I've been wanting to do for a long time.'

'What's that?' asked Raff.

'Just sell books,' answered Ma Carney. 'With all this money I'll be able to go to a proper sale and buy a whole pile of second-hand books, and that will start me off in business . . . that is, after I've rewarded you boys and the old lady who gave you the stuff.' She gave them a generous handful of money each, and a five pound note for Mrs Finch.

'Chai,' begged Tommy Mac, '*you* go round to Mrs Finch, will you? I've got something very important to do.' He shot off to the dog stall.

'You nearly missed him,' announced the dog-seller. 'Been a queue of folk a mile long for this brown pup; had a job 'anging on to 'im, like.'

'Oh aye,' said Tommy, not believing a word. 'I'll pay for him now then.'

'Forty pence,' said the dog-seller.

'You said twenty-five before.'

'So I did. That clean slipped my mind.' He gave Tommy a malicious glance which was utterly wasted on him.

'And I'll have that white one as well.'

The dog-seller was pleased; he'd been trying to get rid of the brown puppy for weeks—it was extremely ugly—and now he'd sold it and a second one into the bargain.

Tommy could also afford the bus back. He could hardly wait to get home.

'What have you got there, our Tommy?' asked his mother when he arrived.

'Two pups, Mam.'

'Oh well, put them out in the back yard for now lad; your tea's catching a cold.'

Later Maureen came in from the loo. 'Hey Mam,' she said, 'what are those two tatty dogs doing in our yard?'

'They're Tommy's new pups.'

'Ugh! They look 'orrible. What're you going to call them, Tommy?'

'Dunno yet.'

'What about Rex and Spot?'

'Aah, don't be soppy, our Maureen. I've just decided; the white one's Count and the other one's Dracula.'

'Oh well, that brown one's ugly enough anyway,' Maureen snorted.

But Tommy by this time was out in the yard with his dogs and couldn't hear her.

## 3. The Newcomer

The third house down from Number Seven was empty. It was a corner house with a cobbled back yard. In place of net curtains and potted plants hung an assortment of corrugated iron and old doors. The back of the house, however, was not so well fortified, and for some time Tommy Mac and his gang had been using it as their headquarters. As headquarters go, it was quite luxurious: there was running water, a highly decorative loo (white lilies on a blue background) and two comfortable leather armchairs, left behind by the previous tenant.

Tommy Mac sprawled in one of the chairs discussing the size of the gang with Raff and Chai. Three members were usually enough, but sometimes they felt that a fourth would be useful. Rock O'Shaughnessy was the extra they would have liked, but Rock was busy following Whacker Casey's gang around and it looked as if Whacker Casey was going to get him.

'What's Whacker Casey got that we haven't?' asked Raff.

'Dunno,' said Chai, 'his headquarters isn't as good. It's his dad's bicycle shed and they're always being told to clear out of it.'

'He gets into loads of trouble at school,' suggested Tommy.

'Not more'n you,' said Raff loyally.

'No, I suppose not.'

'Well then?'

'I reckon I know why,' decided Chai, 'he's got transport.'

'Transport!' Raff scoffed. 'That rotten old bike! The rust falls off in binfuls every time he gets on it.'

'Still, it moves doesn't it? And we haven't got anything that moves,' argued Chai.

Tommy Mac considered. 'We haven't got transport yet,' he said, 'but we will have. I think you've hit on it there, Chai. Transport's pretty important. I don't know how we've got along without it before.'

'What do you mean, Tommy, "we will have"?' asked Raff with interest.

'Come on and I'll show you,' said Tommy, importantly.

They visited the highly decorative loo in turn, locked up, and set off down Paradise Way in the wake of their leader. Tommy led them down to the iron bridge and along the dock road. At last they came to a high embankment. An imposing railing guarded it. Beyond the railing was the base of a pram.

'There!' said Tommy. 'Transport!'

'But you can't get *that*!' exclaimed Raff. 'There's a six hundred foot drop at the bottom of that embankment.'

'Two hundred,' said Tommy.

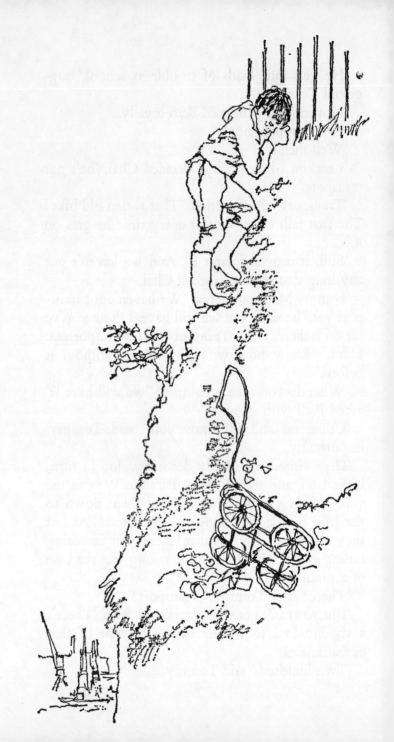

'It's dangerous,' Chai added.

'It's dangerous leaving pram wheels there; they'll drop over one day and kill somebody. I'm going over to get 'em,' Tommy announced.

'Oh gosh!' said Raff and Chai together.

They looked up and down the street to see if there were any police around, then they hoisted Tommy over the railing. He sat down and, using his heels as brakes, gingerly edged his way down towards the pram base. He reached it and grabbed hold of the handle; a shower of stones and miscellaneous objects cascaded over the edge of the embankment into the dock below. He held on to a withered elderberry bush until the avalanche subsided, then he shuffled backwards up the slope.

'Easy,' he boasted as he flung himself and the wheels back over the railings.

The next step was to find a suitable piece of wood to make a seat. They scavenged around for the rest of the morning but could find nothing.

'I know!' said Raff. 'My mam put a burnt ironing board out for the bin-men, only they didn't take it.'

'Then why didn't you say so sooner?' snapped Tommy.

'Never thought of it.'

The burnt ironing board was still there. It was just long enough to seat four. They returned to headquarters with their finds.

'Undo the wheels while I put a notice on the door,' commanded Tommy. With a piece of red chalk he wrote:

NO MORE MEMBUS ALOUD

'What have you written that for?' asked Raff.

'Cos.'

'Cos what?'

'Cos if Rock O'Shaughnessy thinks we don't want him, it'll make him want to join,' explained Tommy Mac.

'Oh,' said Raff admiringly.

The wheels were fixed to the base of the pram in a most peculiar way. They refused to come undone and the gang grew hot and frustrated.

'I'll get our Stevey to make the go-cart,' said Tommy. 'He's got the tools.'

Stevey was off work with a cold. He was sitting with a newspaper in one hand and a glass of ale in the other when Tommy came home.

'Will you make us a go-cart, Stevey?' Tommy asked cautiously.

'No,' answered Stevey without looking up.

'I've got all the parts. You could make it easily; you're strong,' wheedled Tommy.

'No,' said Stevey again.

'Rotten pig,' Tommy thought angrily, but he only said, 'I'll do anything you ask.'

Stevey put the newspaper down and considered. There was a girl in the launderette he'd had his eye on for a whole week. She was a really fancy piece of work, he thought, but she wouldn't tell him where she lived. Stevey was more used to avoiding females than chasing them. He didn't like to be snubbed; it did his ego no good at all. If he could just find out where she lived, he felt he could win her over. He could hang around there in his best clothes, and she'd get a chance to see him as he really was—good looking and 'with it'. He'd even cut his hair if that was what she wanted.

'Alright,' he grunted at last, 'I'll make your bloomin' go-cart if you can find out where Ivy Lunnon lives.'

'Ivy who?' asked Tommy.

'The girl who works in the Park Hill launderette . . . not the old 'un, the young 'un.'

'It's a deal,' agreed Tommy, and promptly vanished.

Mrs Mac, as usual, was in the back kitchen. 'Can I take your laundry, Mam?' asked Tommy.

'What for?' asked his mother; she could never figure out Tommy's ways.

'I just feel like helping,' said Tommy untruthfully.

'Well, it would help,' said Mrs Mac. 'There's a whole load upstairs.'

She collected the washing gratefully and stuffed it into a plastic bag. Tommy Mac trailed down to Park Hill and flung the laundry into a washing machine. He sat down opposite the machine to watch the clothes tossing around. He made bets with himself to see how long it would be before Mr Mac's checked shirt would appear. He had just counted up to thirteen when a peculiar female in a pink nylon overall appeared from a room at the back.

'Ivy Lunnon, I suppose,' thought Tommy.

He regarded her critically. She was thin but shapely in an exaggerated sort of way. Her face was deathly white and two sets of false eyelashes clung to her eyelids. They fluttered over her eyes making vision almost impossible. Beneath her eyes hung yet another set. They looked like tarantulas. Her mouth was covered in some kind of fluorescent grease.

'Blimey!' thought Tommy. 'Our Stevey must be stark raving bonkers, or else he needs an eye test.'

'What's your name then?' he asked nonchalantly.

'What's it to you?' drawled the ghoulish female.

'Just wondered,' said Tommy.

'Cheeky kid! S'Ivy,' she volunteered.

'Do you live round here?' Tommy asked eagerly.

'Happen I do.'

'Where?' Tommy persisted.

'Your washing's done,' Ivy pointed out and disappeared into the back room.

'Females!' thought Tommy despairingly. 'Can't think why anybody bothers with them.'

He raced home, flung the washing into the passage, and ran back to the launderette.

It was now twenty past five and Ivy Lunnon was putting on her coat and chatting to the evening attendant. Tommy waited in a nearby doorway until she had a good head start then he followed her. To his great irritation, she boarded a bus. He had no money, but he leapt on regardless. Eight stops later, Ivy Lunnon stepped off the bus and walked into the Odeon Cinema. *The Four Loves of Yoko Chin*, read Tommy from the billboard. 'Blow!' he cursed under his breath. 'A whole afternoon wasted on that creature.'

The following day he again waited outside the launderette. Ivy Lunnon reappeared wrapped in a fun-fur. She minced off down the road. Wearily, Tommy Mac trailed after her. This time she turned down Fish Street and into Queen's Gardens. She reached a block of flats, teetered up a flight of stone stairs and along a verandah. Then she rang the bell of one of the flats and was admitted immediately.

'Number 73a, Queen's Gardens,' panted Tommy, bursting in on Stevey who was supping ale in the kitchen.

'Oh great! Just shows, everyone has his uses sometimes—even *you*,' Stevey laughed, delighted.

'What about my go-cart?' Tommy asked.

'Oh yeah, that. I'll do it tomorrow; I've got to keep my cold warm tonight.' He flicked the top off another bottle of ale.

Tommy was up early the next morning. Stevey wasn't. Eventually he slumped downstairs, looking haggard. He swayed to the medicine chest and dosed himself liberally.

'Are you going to make it now?' Tommy asked.

'Make what?'

'My go-cart.'

'Urrr,' groaned Stevey. He covered his face with the morning paper and crunched his way through a bowl of cornflakes for what seemed like hours. Finally he lurched out into the back yard and applied himself to the job in hand. With a couple of hard wallops he had the two sets of wheels separated. Yawning vastly, he flung the ironing board upside down, placed the wheels in position and, before Tommy could see how, fixed them on to the board. Still yawning, he produced a penknife from his hip pocket, cut a three foot length from Mrs Mac's washing line and threaded it through two holes he had bored at the front of the go-cart.

'There you are,' he said. 'Now leave me alone for a couple of weeks will you?'

'Stevey, that's great!' said Tommy admiringly. 'You're wasted on the docks.'

'Sure, sure,' said Stevey, 'completely wasted.'

'You should have been a mechanical engineer or something.'

'Or definitely something,' Stevey agreed. He was thinking of Ivy and a new flowered shirt with tie to match he'd seen in Bogans.

Tommy left him thinking and bowled grandly down Paradise Way on his new transport. Deliberately, he turned into Canal Street; Rock O'Shaughnessy lived in Canal Street. He always played 'out' in the mornings as Tommy Mac very well knew. This morning was no exception and Rock was playing nine-pins with a row of milk bottles. Tommy could see him out of the corner of his eye without actually having to turn his head. He rolled smoothly past as if he hadn't noticed. and negotiated the next corner with expert ease. Rock O'Shaughnessy gaped. Tommy Mac, grinning, made for headquarters.

Chai and Raff had lit a fire with wood collected from a nearby demolition site. The room was very cosy. There was half a bottle of lemonade left over from a previous meeting. They shared it out and leant back luxuriously.

'He'll be here soon,' remarked Tommy.

'How can you tell?' Chai wanted to know.

'I just know that's all.'

As usual he was right. There came a timid knock at the door.

'Come in!' yelled Tommy.

Rock O'Shaughnessy appeared through the doorway.

'Oh! S'you!' exclaimed Tommy, faking enormous surprise. 'Take a chair. Make yourself at home.'

Rock O'Shaughnessy sat down, his dark brown skin as shiny as the brown leather. He had been running.

'Thought you'da been out with Casey,' remarked Tommy, swallowing lemonade.

'What—*him*?' snorted Rock.

'Yes. Thought you was in his gang, like.'

'Nah!' said Rock contemptuously.

'I'm surprised to hear you say that.' Tommy was enjoying himself.

'Why, Casey's gang is corny,' went on Rock. 'He's got no good ideas, and when he does get one his boys are never around.'

'Really?' said Tommy.

'You've got to belong to *some* gang though,' continued Rock.

'S'pose so,' conceded Tommy thoughtfully. 'I guess you have.' He moved over to stoke up the fire.

'I don't suppose I could join *your* gang, Tommy?' asked Rock, scratching the woolly black mass of his hair.

'*Our* gang!' exclaimed Tommy. 'Oh, well now, we're a bit full up, aren't we, boys?'

'Yes, a bit full up,' agreed Raff and Chai.

'I'd be jolly useful,' pleaded Rock. 'I can do lots of things.'

'Like what?' asked Tommy.

'Well, I take judo lessons. And I know a bit about boxing; my brother's a boxer.'

The gang was definitely interested. This was something they hadn't known about.

'That *might* come in useful,' said Tommy slowly.

'Might do,' agreed Raff.

'Tell you what,' said Tommy. 'In spite of our notice on the door about no new members allowed, we'll take you on trial for a month. And your gang name will be Nessy.'

'Oh that's great!' cried Nessy, 'I won't let you down, boys, I promise.'

When he had gone, Tommy, Raff and Chai did a war dance round the derelict house. Tommy's jubilant mood vanished, however, when he arrived home and found Stevey waiting for him.

'You *twit*!' Stevey exploded.

'*Me*?'

'Yes, *you*,' yelled Stevey. 'That address you gave me wasn't Ivy Lunnon's at all, it was her boy-friend's, and I nearly got thumped in the eye.'

Tommy was aghast. 'I must have made a mistake,' he mumbled inadequately. 'I'll definitely get it this time—if you give me fifty pence.'

'Fifty!' squealed Stevey indignantly.

'Well I need it; she keeps getting on buses and things—it's expensive.'

'I'll give you fifty pence *after*,' agreed Stevey. He was still very anxious to get to know the glamorous Ivy. Tommy had a bright idea: the finding of Ivy Lunnon's address could be Nessy's first test of worthiness for staying in the gang. Nessy, when he was told, grinned hugely and said that it would be a piece of cake. His long legs swung easily down Paradise Way towards the launderette.

Ivy Lunnon was beginning to get sick and tired of scruffy boys staring at her through the launderette window. This one looked even more doubtful than the others. He was coming in now and he had no dirty laundry with him at all, not even half a sock.

'Get out,' she said unceremoniously.

'Are you the manageress then, girl?' asked Nessy.

'No, I'm not, but I can still throw you out.' Ivy's two sets of eyelashes crumpled together in a tangled mass.

Nessy grinned pleasantly at her and went into the snack bar next door for a Cola. He sat in a window seat. It was five o'clock; in another half hour Ivy would be going home.

Ivy Lunnon was shrewd; she guessed suddenly that Nessy was one of Tommy Mac's friends and that the gang was probably making another attempt to find out where she lived. For the last few weeks she had been 'going off' her current boyfriend—he was getting too bossy by far. Stevey Mac, on the other hand, was beginning to appeal to her. He had thick, curly hair like a pop star. More important, he had a high-powered motor bike.

It was time to leave. She carried her headscarf out into the street, stepped backwards so that she was directly in front of the snack bar window, and made a lengthy job of tying on her scarf. Then she ambled very slowly homewards. Nessy loped along behind her. He was astonished to see her turn along Canal Street; he was walking past his own door. Ten doors further down from his house she stopped, took out a door key and entered, having made quite certain that she had been well observed.

'Cor,' said Nessy to himself, 'fancy me not noticing her before now. S'wonder I didn't see those eyelashes of hers crawling up the street.' He hurried back to the gang with the good news.

'If it's true,' said Tommy cautiously, 'you can stop in our gang.'

On Saturday morning Tommy sat crunching his cornflakes and wondering what to do with the fifty pence Stevey had promised him—if he paid up. After a while, Stevey came thundering down the stairs whistling loudly.

'Hullo, our Tommy,' he said cheerfully.

'Was it . . .?' Tommy began.

'Yeah, sure was. Here you are, our kid, here's a pound.'

'A pound!'

'Yeah, she's a right little raver,' sighed Stevey. 'You done your homework real good. Now clear off and make me a fresh pot of tea.'

Later, Tommy arrived at headquarters with a curious parcel under his arm.

'What is it?' asked Chai.

Tommy unwrapped it and displayed a tin box with a hinged lid. 'It's an oven—for outdoors,' he explained. 'It'll stand on our fire and we can do baked potatoes.'

The oven worked very well. 'New members first,' declared Tommy, handing Nessy a delicious newly baked potato. 'Welcome to the gang, Nessy!'

## 4.   Tommy and the Tramp

The weather had suddenly become very warm and, as one day followed another, it grew even warmer. The gang therefore spent a lot of its time in the water. For five pence the boys could cross the river on *Royal Daffodil*, a large green and yellow ferry, to an open air swimming pool. Nessy soon showed himself to be far and away the best swimmer; he slithered through the water soundlessly, and could dive backwards as well as forwards.

Casey, thin and unsunburnt, sat on the edge of the pool, scowling enviously. Tommy seemed to think that he *owned* Nessy, Casey thought. His own boys hadn't turned up. He was alone and not enjoying himself. On the ferry homewards, he deliberately waylaid Tommy. Tommy was playing ship's captain and was searching for Nessy, who was a dangerous drug smuggler, when Casey popped out from behind a lifeboat and said, 'See you've lost your headquarters.'

'Lost it?' Tommy said. 'How can anyone lose a house! Course we haven't lost it.'

'You have—there's a fella in that house now.'

'You're cross-eyed. There's no fella living in it.'

'No?' sneered Casey. 'Well, why was there

smoke coming out of the chimney? You weren't even there yesterday. And there was a shirt hanging in the yard.'

'There couldn't have been.' Tommy was angry and puzzled.

'Go and see then, why don't you?' Casey taunted. He felt decidedly less miserable now. Wait till that big-headed Tommy Mac saw what he'd got in his fancy headquarters.

The boys enjoyed their nightly chips and pop less than usual. Raff and Chai were certain that Casey had made the whole thing up out of jealousy, and that next day they'd be able to go and hang over his wall and pull tongues at him. Nessy was inclined to agree with them. But Tommy wasn't so sure. He knew Casey too well, and he couldn't imagine him making such a thing up and thus putting himself in danger of being scoffed at afterwards. There *must* be someone in their house. It was too late and too dark to go and investigate that night. They arranged to meet after breakfast.

Mrs Mac was surprised to see Tommy down so early. He had a mournful look about him too. She'd forgotten to give him his medicine for quite a long time. Now she poured out an extra large spoonful. Tommy declared moodily that he wasn't sick, but his mother made him swallow it anyway. She also made him swallow a boiled egg and a hot cup of tea before she allowed him to escape from the table.

Raff, Chai and Nessy were all staring at the chimney of Number Ten; a plume of dark, yellowish smoke was curling out of the chimney.

'Let's creep into the yard,' suggested Tommy. 'You never know, it may only be kids.'

They slithered on their stomachs, commando style, up to the back window and raised themselves up to peer through the glass. There, in Tommy's leather chair, sat an old man. His white hair spread out over his collar. The sleeves of his heavy overcoat had holes at the elbows; the frayed material was bursting like sunflowers round his shirt beneath. His trousers were tied with string at his ankles. He was drinking from a bottle and wiping his mouth on his cuff.

'Gosh!' whispered Tommy. 'A real tramp.'

'What are we going to do?' asked Nessy.

'We'll go in and tell him he's in our house.'

The boys followed their intrepid leader through the back door.

'Ay ay urrrh!' growled the tramp, making the boys jump.

'What are you doing here?' asked Tommy as severely as he could manage. 'This happens to be *our* house.'

The tramp narrowed his eyes. His lower lip hung down, damp with beer. A single yellow tooth jutted out. Chai stepped back two paces towards the door. '*Your* house!' The tramp's voice sounded like an avalanche of gravel. 'Show me the deeds.'

'Deeds?' Tommy looked blank.

'Yes, *deeds* boy, *deeds*. Don't you know what deeds are?'

Tommy didn't.

'Well, boy, deeds are bundles of papers with lots of writing on 'em, saying when the house was built, to whom it first belonged, and who owns it now, and *you* lot certainly don't. Anyway, this place is very much to my liking, so shove off!' He made a threatening movement with his bottle, and Tommy and the boys fled.

As bad luck would have it, Casey was sitting on the kerb as Tommy and his gang came shooting out of Number Ten. 'I told you someone had got your house, didn't I,' he smirked.

Tommy's brain spun round wildly like a catherine-wheel. 'Oh him . . . you mean him? . . . my Uncle Harry. I didn't know you meant *him*. Is that who you meant? He's got our permission, hasn't he boys?'

'Yes, he's got Tommy's permission, didn't realise you meant *him*,' said the gang, somewhat bewildered by this new turn of events.

Casey was stumped at this piece of news. He suddenly remembered that he was supposed to be shopping for a cabbage for his mother.

'Now what are we going to do?' asked Raff as Casey disappeared down the street.

'Dunno,' Tommy admitted. 'We'll just have to get him out.'

'How?' asked Nessy.

'Dunno,' said Tommy again. 'I'll have to think.'

That night Tommy couldn't sleep. He tossed around in his bed under the roof. He listened to Mrs Mac running water in the back kitchen, and the inevitable shudder of the gas geyser. He heard his father locking up and raking out the fire. Finally the house was silent. The old tramp was really poor, thought Tommy. He had nothing decent to wear and nowhere to live. The gang expected him to get the tramp out, but where would the old man go? Tommy tried to imagine how it must feel to be a tramp with no one to feed him, or to give out clean socks, or to ask 'what's the matter?' when he wasn't feeling well. Tommy felt miserable; it was a terrible thing to be alone. It was his duty to help the tramp.

As dawn broke over the grey street, he got up and dressed. His father, who was going off early, was frying his own bacon and eggs. He reckoned Mrs Mac had enough to do during the day. He tossed in an extra egg as Tommy lurched into the kitchen.

'Dad,' said Tommy sleepily, 'have you any clothes you don't want?'

'I'm wearing them, son,' laughed Mr Mac.

'No, really, Dad?'

Mr Mac glanced at his son's serious face. 'Well now, what are you up to this time?' he asked. He poured Tommy a hot cup of tea and listened attentively while Tommy proceeded to tell him all about the tramp.

'Listen, lad,' he said at last, 'there are hundreds of fellows like that. Some of them are genuine and some of them are just bone idle. How do you know this fellow of your's isn't just an old dodger?'

'I'm sure he isn't. But anyway he's jolly poor—he's got newspaper sticking out of his shoes.'

Mr Mac routed out an old pullover which would no longer stretch round his huge chest and gave it to Tommy.

Armed with the pullover and some hastily made

marmalade sandwiches, Tommy set off towards headquarters. The tramp was brewing a thick mixture of tea in a battered saucepan and he growled unwelcomingly as Tommy entered. Tommy produced the marmalade sandwiches and gingerly offered them to him. The tramp eyed Tommy silently and then grabbed the sandwiches. It was amazing, Tommy mused, how a single tooth could work so efficiently; the sandwiches were finished before one could say 'how's your father's mother-in-law'. The tramp studied Tommy again.

'D'you fancy a cup of tea?' he asked unexpectedly. Tommy was gratified but the tea was dreadful. It looked and tasted like hot treacle but it made him feel talkative. He told the tramp all about his gang, and about Casey's gang too. And about telling Casey that he—the tramp—was his Uncle Harry. The tramp chuckled. 'Uncle Harry!' he muttered. He liked that. He chuckled louder. 'You young rascal! You lyin' son of a gun!' Tommy greatly admired the way the tramp spoke. No other grown-up he knew spoke quite like that.

'Where did you live before you came here?' Tommy asked.

'Oh, here and there. Everywhere 'cept Buckingham Palace maybe. You name it, I've slept there.'

'Could we call you Uncle Harry do you think?' asked Tommy hopefully.

'I tell you what,' said the tramp, 'I'd like some more of those marmalade sandwiches. And perhaps half a pound of tea, and some of that there powdered milk—keeps better that does, seeing as how I haven't got a fridge in this 'ere establishment. Then you can call me what the heck you like.'

Tommy agreed joyfully, and sped off to tell the gang.

'Did you get him out?' Chai asked.

'Get him out?' Tommy put on a great air of indignation. 'Certainly not. Just because people don't look posh, doesn't mean one can be rude to them.'

'But what about our headquarters; he's gone and taken it off us.'

'He has *not* taken it off us,' said Tommy with dignity, 'he has merely taken a room. We've got a tenant. Can you think of any other gang around here who's got tenants?'

The boys couldn't. It was certainly a new way of looking at the problem. They never ceased to be amazed at the way Tommy could turn a bad situation into a good one.

As the boys didn't want to disturb their tenant again that day, they went to the park and sat on the swings to talk things over. It was obvious that Tommy couldn't take *all* the marmalade sandwiches; they would have to take turns. Each of them promised to drink at least one bottle of lemonade a day and take the bottle back to the shop. At a penny a bottle that would bring in fourpence a day—nearly enough to buy a pint of milk for a start.

'I can get fivepence for messages,' said Chai eagerly, 'you can buy a couple of eggs for fivepence; eggs is jolly good for you.'

47

'And my dad knows a sailor,' put in Nessy, 'who's always giving him bananas and pine-apple. They don't all get eaten, I could bring plenty.'

'What about you Raff? You ain't said nothing yet,' Tommy said.

Raff looked uncomfortable. His father wasn't doing too good. His mother was always saying how much it cost her to keep them all fed. She said it nearly every day. 'I can't bring nothing,' he said glumly.

Tommy understood. 'It's not just bringing,' he snapped, pretending to sound irritated, 'It's *doin*' as well. That house is a proper mess. You could clean it up a bit, couldn't you?'

'Sure! I could do that easy,' agreed Raff happily. 'I've done plenty of scrubbing and cleaning at our house.'

'Well then,' said Tommy.

'Isn't this exciting!' exclaimed Chai.

The boys' mothers found it less exciting. 'Who *is* this old man?' they wanted to know.

'What on earth is happening to the marmalade?' complained Mrs Mac. 'I only bought this jar on Tuesday and it's half gone.'

'Our Tommy's got a tenant,' Mr Mac laughed.

'A layabout you mean,' grunted Stevey.

'He's *not*!' shouted Tommy passionately. 'He's very, very poor.'

'He's a layabout,' said Stevey again. 'A rotten old layabout who's living off my wages.'

'Your wages!' screamed Tommy. 'You hardly never go to work—layabout yourself!'

'Now then,' interrupted Mrs Mac, 'my marmalade's no joke, our Tommy. I've got enough to feed without finding more for no old man.'

Raff, Chai and Nessy were facing similar trouble. Meanwhile the old tramp was developing a bigger and better appetite every day. He had grown tired of marmalade sandwiches and was now demanding bacon ones. He declared that he was sick and tired of drinking milk and preferred coffee—freshly ground. He swore that these were the worst digs that he had ever had the misfortune to come across. Tommy, anxious to keep his tenant happy, took on a paper round. It meant getting out of bed an hour earlier, but he still believed that Uncle Harry, as they now called the tramp, needed him. He had read somewhere that old people often became cantankerous and that it was not really their fault. Tommy was determined that the tramp should have the best.

Casey, who was not actually dying of curiosity but beginning to feel quite poorly with it, had decided to see for himself what Tommy's Uncle Harry was like. He had mustered together two of his gang, Dyson and Akim. They proceeded to the back kitchen window of Number Ten with extreme caution and peered through it. There sat Tommy Mac's uncle. He was fast asleep surrounded by beer bottles. The jersey Tommy had given him was covered in tomato soup stains, bread crumbs and cigarette ash. Clutched in one hand was a 'Sporting Pink', and his lower lip, which seemed to hang down nearly to his chest, vibrated rhythmically with his thunderous snores.

'Look at that!' sniggered Casey gleefully. '*That* is Tommy Mac's important Uncle Harold! He's a dirty old tramp!'

Dyson and Akim giggled.

'Oh my!' mocked Casey. 'He looks like the bloomin' Duke of Beresford. Take a load o' them there Bond Street clothes. Don't you just wish you could afford a jacket like that?'

Still giggling, they crawled out of the yard.

At six o'clock, Casey hung around McCann's fish shop. It was Friday night. The Macs always had fish and chips on Friday nights and Casey had not long to wait before Tommy came swinging down the road.

'Hiya,' greeted Casey.

Tommy ignored him. This was the custom.

'Saw your uncle today,' said Casey casually.

50

'Been telling lots of people about him. There was a lot of kids down on the iron bridge this avvy. Been telling them all about your uncle. They was very interested.'

Tommy grinned. He felt as if he had swallowed a firework. His grin grew wider.

'He's nothing but a dirty old tramp,' taunted Casey.

'Wake up!' barked Mrs McCann. 'Have you come here for fish or a chat?'

The boys placed their orders and, with fish and chips stuffed inside their jackets, faced each other again on the pavement outside.

'Well, that's just where you're wrong,' said Tommy. 'I thought it would fool you. You see, my Uncle Harry's writing a book. He's a famous author, you see. And the book's about tramps, and he said to me it's no use writing a famous book about tramps unless you know what it feels like to be one. So he's *pretending* to be one just so he knows how it feels like. And when he's finished writing his book he's going on a cruise round the world to have a rest.'

'You're a liar,' said Casey uncertainly.

'Oh well, there's only one way to find out in that case. I'll have to arrange a special introduction. Then you can ask my uncle yourself.'

'Alright then,' said Casey unexpectedly. 'I can come now.'

Tommy was horrified; he thought he'd called Casey's bluff.

'I'll have to take the suppers home first. My mam'll be doing an Irish jig.'

'Twenty minutes then,' said Casey. He was being unusually stubborn.

Tommy reckoned that, if he raced, he'd get home and down to the tramp before Casey could get there. But Casey didn't go home at all. He was waiting for Tommy outside Number Ten looking particularly smug. There was no ducking out now. Tommy led the way into the house.

The tramp was indulging in a light supper. He was eating sardines from a tin. He had apparently mislaid the fork Chai had given him and was stuffing them into his mouth with his fingers. He appeared to be relishing his meal greatly. Sardine oil meandered down his bristly chin and on to his scarf.

'Evening Uncle Harry,' said Tommy.

'Oh, wotcher cock,' muttered the tramp.

'This is Casey,' said Tommy. 'Remember, I told you about Casey. He wants to ask you something.'

Tommy gave a meaningful look but the tramp wasn't looking.

'Are you Tommy's uncle?' began Casey abruptly.

'Sure,' said the tramp, still not looking up. There was a sardine stuck in the corner of the tin. He hooked it out with a tie-pin.

'And are you writing a book about tramps?' persisted Casey.

The tramp looked up, surprised. He caught sight of Tommy who was pulling frantic faces behind Casey's back. 'I am, as it happens,' replied the tramp casually. 'Why do you want to know?'

Casey was dumbfounded. He was both furious and mortified. But the tramp liked his new role and warmed to the subject.

'I've been busy at it for weeks now. As a matter of fact I hardly had time to stop for this small repast.' He flung the empty sardine tin into the fireplace and transferred the sardine oil from his chin to his jacket sleeve. 'All these bits of paper you perceive 'ere 'ave got writing on 'em.' He tossed a pile of papers to one side. They were covered liberally with the names of horses, all of which had let him down.

'Well I did tell you, didn't I?' said Tommy. 'I did tell you that he was my uncle, and he was writing a book, and that he's famous.'

'Now then, Thomas boy, don't boast so much. You'll be telling your young friend next about the last book I wrote, when I was obliged to live with a tribe of head-hunters in South America and had to kill a lion single handed when I already had one arm broken. It's not right to boast, you know.'

Casey turned white and left with all haste.

'That was great, Uncle Harry. I couldn't have done better myself.'

'Yeah, well . . . I don't like to complain, but you boys aren't really bringing me enough to eat. I'm a big man; eggs and milk aren't keeping me fit. A fellow like me's got to have steak. A bag of coal wouldn't come amiss either.'

The gang was delighted when they heard about the shaming of Casey. They kept asking Tommy to tell it to them again. Nessy rolled round in the gutter like a great black dog and hooted with laughter. But the boys were not so pleased about the tramp's fresh demands.

'My mam's getting really fed up,' grumbled Chai. 'She says she won't give me any more.'

Nessy said that his mother felt the same way.

They certainly couldn't afford to buy him a bag of coal. They all began to wonder how the tramp had managed before he had met them. He was pretty old so he must have had plenty of practice. Tommy tried to stick up for the tramp in the face of this sudden disloyalty but he had the uncomfortable feeling that the others were right. It had certainly messed up their holiday. They were finding that they had no time to go anywhere in case they were late back for the tramp's meals. And, come to think of it, he didn't often say thank you, if ever. He only asked for more and even complained on occasions. Reluctantly, Tommy had to admit that he was beginning to get just a little bit tired of his Uncle Harry. In fact he was getting thoroughly fed up with him.

'Come on,' Tommy decided suddenly. 'Let's go and tell him. I don't care if Casey finds out. We pulled his leg soft and he believed us.'

A most unexpected sight met their eyes as they turned the corner. Outside Number Ten stood a police car with its lights flashing. Instinctively they ducked down behind a wall. A crowd of women had gathered on the pavement, clutching children and shopping bags. Their eyes were riveted on Number Ten.

'What's going on?' Tommy asked.

'Oh, some old fella's squatting in that 'ouse. The police are getting 'im out. Dirty old fella by the sound of it.'

The women shuffled closer to get a better view as two policemen emerged from the house dragging Uncle Harry with them. He was cursing and swearing and calling down all sorts of evil upon the police and the women in the crowd and everyone in general.

'Isn't it awful!' chorused the delighted women, moving closer to see the tramp hustled into the police car. 'Isn't he disgusting!'

The gang felt sorry for Uncle Harry but they were secretly relieved to have their headquarters back to themselves. The following day they made their way to it joyfully, only to find that two workmen were busily engaged in taking down the corrugated iron and replacing it with glass.

'What are you doing!' exclaimed Tommy indignantly.

'Someone's bought this house, nosey. We're doing it up.'

Utterly defeated, the gang went swimming.

## 5. Casey and the Damp Squibs

'We need a terrific lot of money for fireworks this year,' announced Tommy Mac. 'They've gone up something shocking.'

'Well, we haven't *got* a lot, have we?' said Chai.

'And we aren't likely to get a lot, are we?' added Raff.

'I've had my pocket money stopped,' sighed Nessy.

'Why's that then?' asked Tommy.

Nessy grinned widely and scratched his head. 'That Monday I sagged school, Mrs Nosey Lunt saw me down by the iron bridge and she told on me.'

'Oh well, you're daft!' snorted Tommy. 'You should've gone farther off.'

'I wonder if Casey's got much,' said Raff. 'He says he has.'

'Yes, but he's a liar, isn't he, so maybe he has and maybe he hasn't,' Tommy sneered.

'I know!' interrupted Raff. 'We'll all do jobs at home, and work hard, and not get on anyone's nerves, and . . .'

'That's no good,' scoffed Tommy, 'we'd never get enough. The cheapest rocket costs forty pence and them cheap ones fizzle out six inches above the ground.'

The boys looked gloomy. They wouldn't have minded too much if only they could have been sure that Casey's gang wasn't going to out-sparkle or out-bang them.

They drifted into the local snack bar, adopting the manner of cowboys mozing into their local saloon.

'Four Cokes, and line 'em up,' said Tommy.

'What?' asked the girl behind the counter.

'Four Cokes. Are you deaf or something?'

'She's got rubber lugs!' choked Raff.

'Hey, you, are you speaking to me? I don't have to serve you scruff if I don't want to.'

'You do, girl,' said Tommy. 'Your boss is a proper old skinter—isn't he fellas?'

'Worst old skinter round here,' agreed the boys loyally.

'So,' continued Tommy, enjoying this bit of mickey-taking, 'if he was to find out you turned good money away—money what's the same as anyone elses—he'd get dead stroppy with *you*.'

The girl was new at the job and unaccustomed to the gang. She was half afraid that what the gang had said might be true. So she thumped four Cokes onto the counter—making sure to slop a little out of each. Tommy reckoned that was fair do's, but stared at the girl long enough to make her blink.

'We've just wasted the price of four bangers,' observed Chai.

'Not wasted,' scolded Tommy. 'I need a drink to think.' He'd heard Stevey saying that often.

'Well,' grunted Raff, 'I can still only think of doing jobs, and working hard . . .'

'I've got it!' yelled Tommy. 'Why didn't I think of it before?'

'Think of what?' cried the gang.

'Going into business!' exclaimed Tommy.

'Business?'

'Of course! Gosh, it was so easy! Ma Carney does it, and Darky Cohen and Ritzy O'Riley. *Thousands* of them do it.'

'Yes, and they don't have any other job, do they!' gasped Raff.

'And they pay their rents and live off it, don't they!' said Chai.

'And live and eat and everything!' agreed Tommy.

'But what do they sell?' put in Raff, who thought someone ought to be sensible.

The other three regarded him irritably.

'Darky Cohen sells dogs.'

'That's easy,' said Tommy. 'We just go to the dogs' home and offer to sell some of their dogs for them. They should be jolly glad to let us have a few. It would save a lot of dogs' lives because they only have to kill'm when they've got too many.'

Raff wasn't sure they'd be allowed to have even a few dogs. 'Supposing we didn't sell them all in one day,' he said, 'we'd be lumbered with them.'

This was true. Tommy could imagine that his mother would not be very pleased if he brought half a dozen dogs home with him. Count and Dracula might not be very pleased either. Count and Dracula were both good fighters and might easily eat all the profits.

'Well then,' he said, 'what does Ma Carney sell?'

'Junk,' said Chai.

'Exactly, junk, and our house is already full of that.'

'And ours,' chorused the others.

It was a nuisance having to go to school. It wasted a great many valuable business hours. By the time they were let out, their brains were tired from concentrating on useless sums and on writing stupid poems about stupid autumn leaves; stupid because the only objects over ten feet tall in *their* street were lamp posts which didn't have 'leaves of yellow, gold and brown, fluttering gently, gently down,' but only broken light bulbs.

'Where *she* lives they've got trees,' said Nessy.

'Who?' asked Tommy.

'Miss Peterson.'

'Well, *she* ought to write about them, then, and leave us in peace,' decided Tommy.

Wearily, the boys collapsed in Nessy's front room. Nessy's father was on night shift and his mother was out playing bingo. The rest didn't count; the older ones were outside playing in the street and the others were in bed. It was a funny house, Tommy thought; full of the sort of things he didn't have in his. Full was not quite the right word for there was actually very little furniture. There was a large table and enough chairs round it to seat the O'Shaughnessy family. And there was a sink, and a cooker, and a record player. But there were also strange things like African drums, and masks pinned to the walls, and milk bottles on the dresser crammed with plants that Tommy had never seen anywhere else.

'The first thing,' he said, when he had finished staring, 'is to put up our stall where nobody knows us.'

'But why not in Fish Street or Paradise Way?' asked Raff.

'Because Casey'll see it,' said Tommy.

Neither Casey and his gang nor Tommy Mac and his ever wandered more than about ten streets away from their own, except to go to town or to the park or on a special excursion to visit relatives. As far as they were concerned, other areas of the city were like foreign countries. Therefore it wasn't very difficult to find a place for their stall quite near to home. The place they eventually found was in a street lined with partially demolished houses.

'This is jolly handy!' exclaimed Tommy. 'Look at all them planks and bricks.'

'What'll we do with them?' asked Nessy.

'Make a counter, of course.'

'Oh yes! 'cried Nessy. 'And we could build a hut to sit in for when it rains.'

'With seats in it,' said Chai.

The boys marvelled at the fact that they had never before thought of going into business and also at the fact that they had never been in this particular street which was so full of promise and unexplored rubbish.

'And another thing, d'you know what?' added Tommy. 'We could go into the scrap business, too. Look at all those drainpipes and bed irons and old cookers. Gosh! I read once where there was this fella who became a millionaire just because he bothered picking all this sort of stuff up.'

Almost drunk with delight and ambition, the boys wended their way home to supper. Each of them owned a mother who expected that he should show up at meal times, and who thought of things like baked beans and toast and dishes and cookers but never of becoming a millionaire.

The following day was Saturday, the most precious day of the week. Armed with enough junk to fill Woolworths from the front door to the back, the boys set off for their new place, which they had named Jericho. Nessy and Chai lugged the go-cart whilst Tommy and Raff kept an eye skinned for Casey and his lot. 'Probably still soaking in bed,' observed Tommy exhilarated.

In five minutes, the boys had erected a counter and covered it with junk. Nessy, in the background, was taking longer to construct a shelter. He had found an old painting and was busily trying to fix it into the brickwork.

'Makes it look like an office,' he explained.

It was amazing, Nessy thought, the amount of useful objects people leave behind. He had found two kitchen chairs, a bookcase with all the shelves still intact, and a suitcase with only one small hole in a corner.

'Hey Ness, that's gear!' praised Tommy. 'Ritzy O'Reilly uses a suitcase like that when he's packing up.'

By now it was ten o'clock. A drove of housewives with large shopping bags was bearing down

the street. Most of them ignored the boys, but one fat woman came across to the stall, examined it critically, and asked, 'How much's those?'

'The shoes?' asked Tommy. 'Five pence.'

'L'avem for three,' said the fat woman, her face expressionless.

'All right,' Tommy agreed, and business began.

'You should've stuck to five,' said Chai.

'You just don't know about business,' said Tommy scornfully. 'You pretends to want twice as much—make your tickets dearer, like—then one gets the price you really expected.'

'What?' said Chai.

'Never mind, wack,' said Tommy wearily.

At the end of the day the gang had made fifty-five pence. They could hardly believe it.

Sunday, they all agreed, was not a good day for trading, so it was Monday after school when the boys reassembled at Jericho. Tommy had spent Sunday afternoon making treacle toffee. This was one thing he was good at. Charlie had got at the toffee and eaten quite a lot, and Mags and Kate a bit more. Tommy himself had eaten a certain amount but there was still a good deal left. He shared it out into empty margarine containers and arranged them temptingly on the stall.

That day several women came straight up to the stall. They were mainly interested in the clothes and none of them would pay the prices the boys asked. This was really not very surprising as Tommy had priced his father's old raincoat at two pounds fifty, which was not far off the original price.

'I'll give yer twenty-five pence for it,' a woman offered.

'Twenty-five!' This time Tommy was outraged. 'We're not running this business for charity, you know. It's not your bloomin' W.R.V.S. or nothin.'

'No,' jeered the woman, 'charity wouldn't have half that lot!'

'Well, why do you want that coat, then?' Tommy wanted to know.

'Because my 'usband's just started workin' on the bins, you see, and that'd just do 'im a turn.'

Tommy was even more indignant; his father had only recently stopped wearing the coat. 'It's not for sale no more,' he snapped and stalked into the 'office'. In a low voice he said to Nessy, 'You can go out and sell it to the old faggot if you like.' Nessy swung rhythmically up to the stall, hitching up his pants around his thin waist. 'What was it, lady?' he said.

'That coat. I want it for twenty-five pence.'

'Well, who's arguing with yer, Missus?' He wrapped it up. 'Sold to the lady in the big yeller 'at,' he said.

The crowd giggled. The laughter brought more women over to the stall, and the gang was kept quite busy wrapping up goods. They even ran out of newspaper.

Then tragedy struck. A panda car drew up at the kerb and a tall policeman stepped out. At the sight of the uniform the gang stiffened.

'Oh, it's only Constable Jackson,' said Tommy.

Constable Jackson strode slowly round the stall and scrutinised the wares. Nessy disappeared into the office; Chai and Raff rearranged a few things which didn't need rearranging, and Tommy stood and waited for whatever was coming.

'Got a licence, have you?' asked Constable Jackson at last.

'A what?' asked Tommy.

'A street traders' licence; have you got one?' repeated the constable patiently.

'What's that?' Tommy asked.

'Ah well, now, it's a bit difficult to explain. It's just a piece of paper, really, with writing on. Gives one permission to sell in the street.'

Tommy knew that Constable Jackson knew that he hadn't got one, but he said, 'We'll get one then.'

'Sorry, lad, but you're under age.'

'Well, what can we do?' asked Tommy.

'You can close shop and go home. That's all, I'm afraid.'

Constable Jackson was really very fond of the boys. They never gave him any real trouble. Their idea about the stall was really a very good one and, he thought secretly, the law was often pretty mean.

'Come on,' he said kindly, 'put all that clobber into the back of my car and I'll give you a ride home.'

It was November the fifth. Tommy was glum and silent at breakfast. Then his father said, 'There's going to be a huge firework display in the park tonight. Why don't you go there, Tommy?' He knew what his son was fretting about.

'The park!' exclaimed Tommy. 'The park! We wanted it in our own street, same as usual.'

'Now listen, our Tommy, every year some poor kids get burnt up. Nobody thinks it's going to be them. But every kid what gets burnt belongs to *somebody*. That's why the Corpy are putting on their own display. I bet they spends a hundred pounds on *their* fireworks.'

'More like two hundred, Dad,' put in Mrs Mac, 'and it all comes out of our rates, so you go to it, love.'

Tommy thought about this on the way to school. A hundred, or two hundred pounds worth of fireworks! It ought to be jolly good. He went about persuading Raff, Chai and Nessy that it was a cunning idea to go to the park.

As bad luck would have it Mr Jones decided to have an assembly. And as bad luck would have it twice in the same five minutes, Tommy found himself sitting next to Casey.

'Where're you having yours?' Casey hissed.

'Our what?' asked Tommy, acting as dumb as possible.

'Your bonfire.'

'Bonfire did you say? We aren't bothering this year. Going to the park we are.'

'The park!' hooted Casey. 'With all that lot of posh cissys from Childwell? Oh diddums!'

'Well, we just ain't wastin' our money when we can go and see the Corpy's fireworks for free,' said Tommy. 'It's daft to waste money.' Inwardly he was seething, and longing to crush Casey's toes under his boot.

That evening, Mrs Mac got the tea ready early; then she put an extra vest on Charlie.

'Are you coming too?' she asked Maureen and Stevey.

'You must be joking!' laughed Stevey.

67

Maureen didn't think the question needed an answer so she didn't trouble to give one.

'You're not coming with us, Mam, are you?' asked Tommy in consternation.

'Of course I am,' replied Mrs Mac. 'It's dark in that park. And anyway, I want to walk some of the fat off me. Also, you might go and lose our Charlie.'

In a way, Tommy didn't really mind his mother coming, just so long as Casey didn't notice.

'Mam, we'll meet you at the corner,' he said.

'Alright,' said Mrs Mac, 'I've got some stuff to buy anyway.'

As luck would have it for a change, all that Casey saw was Tommy and his gang sloping up the street.

The park was almost pitch dark. Tommy had to admit that it really was quite exciting. In the distance, car lights moved without ceasing. But the trees nearby were dark and ghostly.

'Now you hold on tight, Charlie,' warned Mrs Mac. Her breath was like smoke, and Tommy Mac felt strangely comforted by the presence of her round homely figure. Raff, Chai and Nessy seemed to have the same feeling. They chattered excitedly and ran figure-eights in the black wet grass.

'Give over!' cried Mrs Mac happily.

Against the light of a massive bonfire the boys could make out a crowd of hundreds of people.

'Hey look!' cried Mrs Mac. 'Isn't that the mayor?'

'Dunno, is it?' Tommy wasn't interested in the mayor.

68

'Yes, I'm sure it is. And there's Councillor Bush over there, sitting next to Lady . . .'

She was interrupted by a sudden flash of catherine-wheels. They blazed out the word 'Welcome' and were followed by a burst of applause.

'Gosh!' gasped Tommy.

'Gosh!' said the gang.

'I want to go home!' wailed Charlie, terrified.

'It's alright, love,' comforted Mrs Mac. 'Come under my coat.'

Peering through the buttonhole of his mother's large coat, Charlie watched the next burst of fireworks. A dozen rockets zipped into the sky and burst into a cluster of fairy-like green and orange stars.

'Gosh!' whistled Tommy and his friends once again.

'Tee hee hee!' wheezed Charlie, coming out into the open, no longer scared.

There seemed to be no pause between one lot of fireworks and the next. The gang soon grew tired of saying 'gosh'.

'I ain't never going to buy them from a shop again,' vowed Chai.

'My dad was right, wasn't he!' crowed Tommy.

'Yes, and don't forget we've still got all that money from the stall,' Raff reminded him.

'So we have,' said Tommy absently, as at least twenty Roman candles turned the darkness bright pink.

Meanwhile, back in Paradise Way, a huge bonfire was crackling. It belonged to Casey, Akim and Dyson. There were not many fireworks, just

69

an odd bang here and there, but the flames were fifteen feet high. Doors began to open and angry women and their husbands peered out.

'Get that thing out!' they shouted. 'It's too big, you little hooligans!'

'You'll be cracking our windows,' complained Mr Mac.

In reply, Casey, Akim and Dyson lit sparklers and whooped round their fire like Red Indians. Other children, who had long ago spent their 'Guy' money on sweets, whooped after them. Count and Dracula, shut up in the backyard, howled like a couple of coyotes in pain.

Minutes later a fire engine appeared. Someone had evidently phoned for it.

'Alright, clear off!' shouted the firemen.

They fixed up their hoses, ignoring the rage of the children, the impolite criticism, and the odd lump of wood that came flying their way, and they squirted Casey's bonfire out of existence. 'And I should think so!' snorted the Paradise Way grown-ups. 'Little hooligans!'

At ten o'clock—as late as that—Mrs Mac and her brood came joyfully down the street. They were eating fish and chips.

'What's this, then?' asked Mrs Mac. 'All this mess here?'

A sodden black mass blocked the centre of the road.

'Bet I know what it is!' exploded Tommy; 'it's Casey's bonfire.'

'Oh, I bet it is!' cried the others, falling about in ecstasy.

70

'Ah, poor kids,' sympathised Mrs Mac kindly. 'You are a mean lot.'

'Well, Mam, Casey's so big-headed,' defended Tommy.

'And you're not?' she asked. 'Come on, villain,' she laughed, giving Tommy a friendly thump around the head.

'See you tomorrow,' Tommy called after his friends.

# 6. Tommy Takes an Unexpected Trip

It was playtime, and old Miss Bundy was on duty. This was always a good time because Miss Bundy loathed playground duty and spent most of it talking to the 'Biscuit Lady', instead of walking around as she was supposed to do.

Whenever Miss Bundy was on duty there were always plenty of fights. Today was no exception; fights were taking place all over the playground. Miss Bundy's duty always fell on a Wednesday, so Wednesday had become known as 'clobber day'. All grievances were fought out on this day.

Casey had a boiling hot grievance: 'I bet it was your dad brought out that fire engine,' he fumed.

'Brought it out for what?' asked Tommy Mac.

'You know very well for what,' said Casey.

'I don't. I don't know what you're talking about,' lied Tommy.

'Yes, you do!' bellowed Casey. 'I'm talking about our bonfire. It was a smashing one and your dad had it put out.'

'Can you prove it?' taunted Tommy.

Casey couldn't. It could have been any one of about fifty people but he preferred to think that Tommy's father was the ratter. He struck out at

Tommy who raced nimbly up the fire escape. This was forbidden, but he climbed up nevertheless. Casey chased after him and grabbed a handful of Tommy's jersey.

'It *was* your dad, wasn't it?' threatened Casey.

'Listen you, shrimpy! My dad has more to do with his time than to rat on a little scruffer like you and your scooty bonfire.'

Casey made a wild lunge and Tommy Mac fell straight off the fire escape.

The whole school sped screaming to the spot. Casey stood rooted to the steps, and Miss Bundy stumbled, gasping, across the playground. Tommy lay where he had fallen, a ghastly expression on his usually ruddy face. A bone which should have been at the back part of his arm now bulged grotesquely at the front.

'Ow, ow!' screamed Denise Davenport. 'Ow, I'm going to be sick.'

'Shut up!' snorted Tommy. 'Will you shut it! It's my arm not yours.' And then he fainted clean away.

'Gosh!' gasped the children, several of them grinning wildly.

Miss Bundy hadn't the faintest idea what to do, except to send a child post haste for Mr Jones.

The headmaster marched across the playground, looking grim. *He* knew exactly what to do. First of all he had the children lined up and back into class before they could say 'Is it time? Has the bell gone?' And secondly he hammered on his own office window and bellowed to his secretary to phone for an ambulance.

Tommy Mac came to his senses on the way to hospital. Mr Jones was looking down at him.

'How did it happen boy?' he asked.

Tommy tried to remember and then when he did he replied, 'Can't remember, sir.'

'Can't you!' snorted Mr Jones, but not too crossly, and not too believingly, either.

Quite suddenly, Tommy fainted again. When he came round for the second time Mr Jones had gone and, instead, his mother was staring at him.

'Oh, Tommy, you did give us a turn!' she cried.

'Where am I?' he asked.

'Don't you know?' asked Mrs Mac, getting all worked up again. 'That young teacher of yours, Miss Bate, the one what does the piano on the concerts, she came hammering on our door to say you'd got taken bad. I was just doing the tea and I dashed out. She gave me a lift in her car—oh, she's a proper nice girl, she is—and she brought me up on the lift and she had a look at you, too, only you weren't conscious then.'

'But where *am* I, Mam?' asked Tommy again. The pain in his head and in his arm was making him feel dizzy.

'You're in the "Children's",' snuffled Mrs Mac.

'Hospital?'

'Yes,' said Mrs Mac, with an enormous blow into her handkerchief.

Tommy lay for a long time wondering about that. When he tried to look at his mother she seemed to be no longer there; there was only a girl in a purple uniform and a man in white. They were wheeling him, he thought, down a long corridor.

74

He could see enormous lights, bigger than street lights, shining down over him, and there were voices all the time. Then came a lovely dream of pillows and warm blankets. He was drowning in the blankets and sinking lower and lower but he was too warm to worry. It didn't do any good to worry, but one thing did puzzle him: although he was falling fast and pulling the pillows after him, the girl in the purple uniform wasn't falling at all and yet she was always there. 'I must ask her how she manages that, later,' Tommy decided. Then came a dream full of pleasant smells, the smells of bacon and toast. And there were sounds of teacups being rattled. Quite suddenly Tommy opened his eyes and saw a trolley full of breakfast, and several nurses grinning at him. The room was full of beds, and the beds were full of children.

'Good job it's your left arm, isn't it!' laughed a nurse named Kelly.

Then Tommy noticed that his arm was encased in plaster about two feet thick.

'Go on,' jeered Kelly, 'it's only half an inch thick, if that.'

For answer, Tommy did his famous squint act.

'Oh don't!' shrieked Kelly. 'You're revolting.' She gave him a cup of tea and cut his toast into fingers.

'Hit your head then, did you?' she asked.

'I dunno,' munched Tommy. 'Can't remember.'

'Well, you must have done,' Kelly went on chattily. 'Dr Somani missed his supper on account of you, you know.'

'Tough luck,' said Tommy. 'Is there any more toast?'

Kelly supplied him with more toast and a banana. 'But do you know what I think?'

'No,' said Tommy, unzipping his banana.

'I think you were only kidding. I never saw anyone healthier than you.'

Tommy Mac was insulted. 'I think I'm going to faint again,' he moaned.

'Yes I know,' sniggered Kelly, 'after you've finished that banana!'

At that moment Sister appeared on the ward and Nurse Kelly bustled off.

Meanwhile, Raff, Chai and Nessy were having great sport with Casey. They had heard from Mrs Mac that Tommy was not seriously injured but they were determined that Casey should not know about this just yet.

'Yes, they think he's going to die,' they were saying.

'Well, I never done it,' moaned Casey.

'You *did*!' accused Denise Davenport. 'We all *saw* you, you dreadful beast.' She began to cry again for the umpteenth time. She was thoroughly enjoying herself.

'Oh, for goodness sake,' sighed Raff, 'take your box of paper hankies and push off.'

'How dare you talk to me like that when I'm so upset,' gasped Denise Davenport, but she moved off in search of a more sympathetic audience.

That morning at Assembly, Mr Jones decided to say a few short prayers for the recovery of Tommy Mac. The children prayed, and glared at Casey, all at the same time. Then Raff began to feel just a bit sorry for him, so he said, 'Of course, doctors are so clever these days, they might just save him.'

'D'you think so?' said Casey eagerly.

'Well, *I* couldn't say, could I, but they might just.'

Without Tommy, the gang felt oddly lost. 'Be nice to go and have a look at him, wouldn't it?' said Chai.

'S'not allowed.' Nessy knew that from the time when his brother had broken his leg.

'Bet he wants sweets and things,' Chai went on.

'Yes, bet so.'

They strolled aimlessly down to the iron bridge and studied a grain ship being unloaded.

'Wouldn't bother with that job, would you?' said Chai.

'Course I jolly well would,' whooped Nessy, hanging bat-like on the railing and regarding the shore some seventy feet below. 'They gets about a hundred pounds a week, they do.'

'Don't talk so daft!' jeered Raff. 'Course they don't.'

'I read it in the *Echo*.'

'Since when did you learn to read, Rock O'Shaughnessy?' sniggered Raff. 'If that was true, Stevey Mac would be belting down Paradise Way in a Rolls, and he ain't, is he!'

'No, he's only got a second-hand motor bike with permanent L plates on it,' laughed Chai.

But suddenly the boys got tired of ragging each other.

'Let's go and see him,' decided Raff.

'I just told you, it's not allowed. Kids aren't allowed.'

'Well, we don't know that, do we?' said Raff.

'No, we never heard of that rule, did we?' added Chai.

Nessy grinned. 'Let's go and get him some liquorice shoelaces.'

'And some comics,' shouted Raff, beginning to run.

They arrived at the hospital just before visiting time. A large crowd of parents and relatives were waiting at the gate. They were all armed with carrier bags and parcels. Raff had a carrier, too.

'Now we just walk in with this lot,' he reminded the others. 'Just look normal.'

At that moment, the porter in the lodge opened the gate and the crowd clattered into the hospital and down the corridors. They were like an army on the march. No one spoke; all were determined to be first at the ward doors.

Raff, Chai and Nessy arrived at the door of Nightingale Ward. Fortunately, the nurses had made themselves scarce. They usually did this when parents were around.

'Remember,' said Raff, 'don't look soft. Don't look as if you ain't supposed to be here.'

They swaggered into the ward. Tommy, who was not expecting anyone for the afternoon visit, gaped.

'We've brought you stuff,' announced Raff, depositing the carrier.

'Oh great!' exclaimed Tommy. He made a

swift appraisal of the contents of the carrier. 'Hey, thanks,' he said.

'We've got Casey as scared as a chicken for the chopper,' Raff informed him.

'Why?' Tommy asked.

'Well, he thinks he pushed you.'

'Does he?' laughed Tommy.

'And your girlfriend, Denise Davenport, is doing her nut. Bet you'll end up marrying her the way she's going on.'

'Bet I'll go into a monastery first,' wheezed Tommy Mac, rolling around the bed with laughter.

'And we said prayers for you, too,' Chai said.

Tommy was impressed at that. He could just imagine the whole school being forced to pray for him.

'Does your arm hurt?' asked Nessy, suddenly serious.

'Dunno, can't feel a thing,' admitted Tommy truthfully. 'I wish it was my right arm then I wouldn't be able to write or do nothing for the rest of term.'

'Well, you never do anything anyway, do you!' chided Raff.

He was rudely interrupted by a harsh voice. 'You there . . .' It was Sister. 'What do you think you're doing?'

'Visiting our friend,' explained Raff innocently.

'But children aren't allowed in here. Didn't you know?' snapped Sister crossly.

'Oh no! We didn't know,' gasped Raff. 'We didn't know that.'

Sister was momentarily stuck for words. 'Well, you'd better leave now,' she said, somewhat lamely.

'See you, boys,' grinned Tommy, 'and ta.'

'All you need is a bit of cheek and a gormless face,' laughed Raff as they strutted out into the street, their mission accomplished.

Tommy was beginning to enjoy hospital, and the attention he was receiving from his family, when he was suddenly and unceremoniously evicted. That is to say, Dr Somani nodded at him briefly in passing and said, 'You can go home tomorrow, Thomas.'

Seeing his stricken expression, Nurse Kelly nipped back to talk to him afterwards.

'Well, it's not an hotel, you know,' she said.

'But I'm still ill,' complained Tommy.

'Go on! You can sit at home just as easily as in here. In fact,' she went on maliciously, 'you could sit in school—it's only your arm.'

Tommy was thinking of Casey. 'I won't have to go *straight* back to school, will I?' he asked.

'I don't see why not,' laughed Kelly. 'Dr Somani says you can.'

Tommy looked mournful.

'Anyway,' Nurse Kelly said, suddenly getting business-like, 'Out Patients is bulging with kids just waiting to leap into your bed.' And she departed to see if there was any tea left in the pot.

Tommy walked slowly into school. With the help of Maureen's latest face powder he looked extremely pale. At every third step he drew in his breath sharply and gasped in pain. But, unfortunately, his antics were of no avail. As soon as Casey saw that Tommy Mac was not dead but actually back in school, his remorse vanished. Denise Davenport, bored with weeping, glared in an unfriendly fashion at him.

The final indignity came when Mr Jones bellowed, in public, 'Mac, are you coming into class or are you going to sleep where you are?'

Tommy brushed Maureen's powder off his face. It stank, anyway. Then he lumbered into first lesson.

## 7.   The New Leaf

It was twenty past nine—not late by Tommy
Mac's standards, but nevertheless late by Mr Jones'
standards. The headmaster just happened to be
coming down the corridor as Tommy Mac
slipped through the school doorway.

'Ah, good morning, Mac,' he boomed. 'What was
it this morning? Fog? No, it couldn't be that—too
windy. I know! You were helping half a dozen old
ladies to cross the road and they walked so slowly
that it took half an hour to get them all across.'

Tommy rather liked that one—he could just
imagine it. But he said, 'No sir, please sir, I'm
sorry I'm late, sir.'

'No need to be sorry, Mac my boy; I get quite
lonely around tea-time, you know, with all the
children gone—you can stay behind with me and
keep me company for half an hour.'

'Yes, sir,' muttered Tommy, looking indignantly
at a picture of 'Baa Baa Black Sheep' behind Mr
Jones' head and wishing that he were grown up.
At twenty past nine—if he were grown up—he'd
be tearing down a motorway in a big lorry, or
eating bacon and eggs in a transport caff.

'Well, go on boy, before you fall asleep again.
Go and annoy poor Miss Peterson.'

Released, Tommy ran down the corridor and burst into class.

'Oh no,' groaned Miss Peterson. 'I really thought you were going to do us the honour of not appearing today.'

Tommy grinned dutifully and collapsed noisily on to his chair.

'Tommy,' whispered Raff, 'we're going to do a school play. Miss is going to choose us after break.'

'Huh!' Tommy grunted.

'Aren't you keen then?' Raff wanted to know.

'Not specially—dressed up like a lot of twits, jumping around—no, not specially.'

'Miss! Tommy Mac's talking,' shrilled Denise Davenport.

'Tommy!' cried Miss Peterson, exasperated. 'Haven't you even got your arithmetic book out yet? You really are hopeless,' she went on and on. 'If you can't behave better than this you simply won't be in the play, and then your mother will be disappointed.'

Denise Davenport smirked and flicked her ginger ringlets back off her shoulders.

'Miss, he's still smiling,' she added.

'That's enough, Denise. Come along children, find page twenty-three.'

Tommy Mac determined to get Denise Davenport at lunch time and push her down the nearest grid. He reckoned it would only count as manslaughter. She'd been driving him to violence all term. The story would be in all the papers . . .
*Girl with ginger ringlets found suffocated down grid.*

*A boy named Tommy Mac is believed to be helping police with their enquiries. Tommy Mac is a tall handsome boy; fond of dogs, kind to his mother, clever at . . .* The bell rang for play and Miss Peterson sped off to the staff room for her cup of tea. Denise Davenport, sensing danger, asked the art teacher if she might do a job for her and didn't come out into the playground. But Tommy Mac had forgotten her for the time being. The relief of being out in the fresh air blotted out the memory of the last lesson as if it had never happened. He spent the all-too-short playtime fighting with Whacker Casey.

'I saw your dog yesterday,' sneered Casey, 'that brown thing with the mouldy hair stuck all over it.'

That did it. Tommy flung himself furiously on top of Whacker and brought him down on to the ground. Whacker was delighted. He caught hold of Tommy's hair and pulled hard. But they had only just got underway when Miss Ford, who always interfered when she was on duty, separated them. When she had moved off, they re-positioned themselves behind the toilet wall and set upon each other with renewed energy. Raff and Chai stood by and cheered lustily. Dyson and Akim booed. Both Whacker's knees were pouring blood, whereas only one of Tommy's was bleeding. Tommy Mac manoeuvered himself onto the back of his opponent's neck.

'Say you're sorry you insulted my dog. Go on, say you're sorry you cast aspersions on him.'

Whacker wouldn't; his mouth was full of grit

84

and therefore he couldn't. He was saved mercifully by the bell.

'See you later, Whacker,' said Tommy cheerily.

'OK, Tom.'

'I haven't finished with you about what you called our dog.'

'OK, Tom.'

They marched to their separate classes, glowing with good health.

Miss Peterson had a list. Everyone had to be in the school play—good, bad and indifferent. By the time Tommy had washed the blood off his knee, she had chosen half the cast.

'You'll have to be a shepherd,' she told him wearily. 'Have you got a dressing gown?'

'A dressing what?' Tommy asked.

'Oh never mind,' sighed Miss Peterson, 'I'll lend you something. You can bring sandals and a stick I presume?'

'Yes, miss.' He wasn't positive about the sandals, but he was quite sure about the stick.

He wouldn't mind being a shepherd. It wasn't a big part, but he'd get the most out of it. He remembered reading somewhere that lots of the famous stars started off with only one line to say. They said it so well that everyone noticed them and not the other people in the play who had big parts. Tommy Mac could easily imagine how everyone in the audience would clap and cheer when they heard him say his small part, and then listen, bored stiff, to James Mortimer who had half a book to learn. Miss Peterson probably thought she'd belittled him when she gave him a small part, but she was going to be jolly surprised. Tommy Mac sank into a deep well of thought. He was filled up to his ears with a strange new feeling—he was going to turn over a new leaf and behave and do everything right. Yes, that's what he'd do; he'd behave himself and be good, just like James Mortimer who sat like an effigy of a Red Indian god with one finger permanently fastened to his mouth.

A voice from a long way off was calling to him. It grew louder and louder.

'Tommy!' It was Miss Peterson.

'Sorry, miss, were you talking to me?'

The class rocked with merriment.

'Not *talking* to you Tommy; for the last ten minutes I've been shouting at you to go and lie down over there and wait for the angel.'

'Oh yes, Miss Peterson, certainly, I'll do that right away.'

There was a stunned silence as Tommy Mac took his place on the floor, with his arm flung dramatically across his face. Miss Peterson wavered uncertainly and then called, 'Angel!'

In tripped Denise Davenport, arms akimbo, a pious expression on her pasty face.

'Fear not!' she shrieked.

Tommy winced, but remembering his new leaf, obligingly struck an exaggerated pose of utter astonishment and awe. He continued to strike his pose of utter astonishment and awe so long and so violently that Miss Peterson had to intervene.

'Tommy!' she begged. 'This is only a half hour play; there just isn't time to spend ten whole minutes of it carrying on like that. This scene is supposed to be about an angel appearing to a group of shepherds—not an exhibition of wrestling in a stadium.'

With an effort, Tommy controlled himself. He strode manfully across the classroom in search of the stable, resisting the very strong temptation to step on the angel's dress.

'I had no idea it could be so hard,' said Tommy as he strolled home with Raff at lunch-time.

'What could?' Raff said.

'Turning over new leaves.'

'Why? Is that what you're turning over?'

'Yes, didn't you notice then?'

'I thought you was acting a bit funny,' observed Raff.

'Well, I'm not used to doing it.' Tommy felt disgruntled. 'It's much harder than you think. I bet *you've* never tried.'

'S'not worth it. You'd wear yourself out for nothing and nobody'd notice 'cos they've got used to thinking you're always like you usually are, and they just wouldn't notice you not being like it for a few days.' Sometimes Raff showed surprising wisdom in the ways of the world.

Tommy was irritated. 'Well, I'll go on trying it till tea-time anyway,' he threatened.

He returned to school in a fierce mood of determination. He arrived five minutes before the bell. His hands and face were scrubbed. His hair was plastered flat around his ears. Mr Jones stared, then recognising him, raised his eyebrows to a great height and smiled mysteriously.

There was no play rehearsal in the afternoon. It was Art and Craft for the first and second periods. This was a good lesson in which to practise new leaves because it was Tommy's favourite subject—his only favourite subject as it happened. He was making a crocodile. It was an excellent crocodile, he thought. It was made of lots of beer bottle tops, painted green. Miss Peterson said that she thought it was revolting—which meant it was half way to being a success.

'I've brought some teeth for it this week, miss,' Tommy announced.

'Really?' said Miss Peterson. 'Sylvia, take the register down to Mr Jones, there's a good girl.'

'It's an old comb my Mam didn't want no more. It'll make smashing teeth.'

'Denise and Sandra, will you give out the scissors to the boys and the paint and water jars over there to the girls.'

'I need some glue,' Tommy persevered.

'What for?' asked Miss Peterson, looking hot and vaguely bothered.

'To stick his teeth in with.'

'Whose teeth?'

'My crocodile's.'

'Oh that!' said Miss Peterson. 'Do sit down, Tommy, you're dripping green paint everywhere, and I've only got one pair of hands.'

'Oh, I didn't notice—I'm sorry, miss. I bet if you had hands growing out of you all over it would be jolly useful.'

He sat down meekly. For the second time that day Miss Peterson looked at him suspiciously. She hurriedly gave him some glue.

Tommy felt inexplicably content. The comb his mother had given him was a white one, or rather it had started its days white. Meticulously, he snapped it into pieces. With the precision of a surgeon he bored holes in the crocodile's mouth

and glued a tooth into each cavity. The effect was terrifying. Finally, he produced a torn red balloon from his pocket and stuck it down the animal's throat; it made an admirable tongue. Tommy was stunned; he had never made anything as good in his life. He couldn't take his eyes off if.

He was taken by surprise when the bell rang for Writing; usually the afternoon seemed interminable. He glanced round to see what the other children had made. Raff had constructed a house from a shoe box. The windows were crooked and ten times larger than the door and although he had painted roses on the walls, it still looked exactly like a shoe box. Most of the girls had, predictably, painted fairies and fashionable ladies. Chai had made quite a decent tortoise. There was no doubt Tommy's crocodile was the best.

'Write about what you've made,' Miss Peterson said, and settled down to read what appeared to be a letter.

Still in a good humour, Tommy wrote,

'today i hav mad a crokerdial. my dad hoo drinks a lot gav me the botel tops to mak it with. it is sicksteen inches long and has teeth mad out ov a oeld coemb wich my mam kinly gav me. i wuld like to do a job making crokerdials wen i grow up becos that is wot im best at doing. they wuld probly cum in yousful as decorashuns on bildings, or uther things like bildings.'

He broke off to think what to write next. At that precise moment, Denise Davenport knocked the crocodile off Tommy's desk and stood on it. Deathly white, Tommy leapt to his feet and grabbed wildly at her ringlets.

'You're a wicked pig!' he screamed.

'Ow! ow!' howled Denise Davenport.

'Stop it, stop it!' shouted Miss Peterson.

'She did it on purpose; she's the most horriblest person I've ever known in my whole life; she needs hanging!' Tommy was getting hysterical.

Miss Peterson rushed to the rescue but Tommy couldn't be silenced.

'She's insane with jealousy—just because she

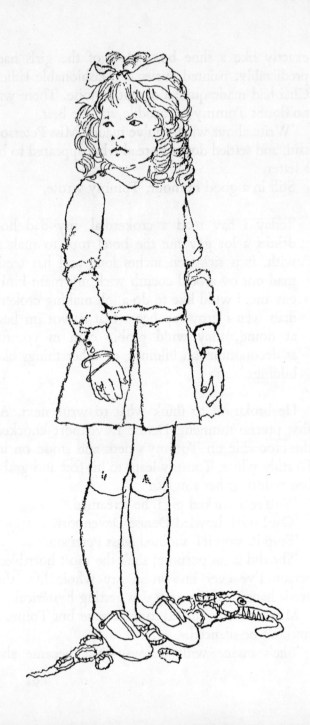

saw I'd made something good and all she can do is draw rotten fairies.'

'Ow! ow! Let go, my hair's going to come out,' screamed Denise, also getting hysterical.

'What is it?' thundered Mr Jones, appearing through the doorway at all speed.

Miss Peterson explained as well as she could over the rumpus.

'Down to my room, boy,' commanded Mr Jones.

Tommy Mac sat in the 'question' chair opposite Mr Jones; the injured crocodile lay on the desk between them. Mr Jones stared at it and said nothing. He continued to stare at it and say nothing for quite some time; then he said, 'Can you make me one?'

'What?' said Tommy.

'I said can you make *me* a crocodile like this one?'

'Yes sir, easily sir,' said Tommy, surprised and gratified.

'I'll bring my own bottle tops,' grinned Mr Jones, 'and you can make it down here tomorrow afternoon. At the same time you can repair the damage to your own.' He put the crocodile in his drawer. 'Now all that remains to be done is to apologise to Miss Davenport and the matter's closed.'

Denise was still whimpering when Tommy got back to class.

'Sorry,' he said to the nearest cupboard. But the wretched Denise ignored him.

'I wouldn't even bother blocking the grids with her,' said Tommy to Raff. 'She's not worth it.'

He was in a great humour again.

## 8. The Enthusiastic Shepherd

The time for the Christmas play was drawing near. Tommy's part had been cut somewhat. In fact, it had been cut so much that it was now almost non-existent. At first he hadn't minded because those children who hadn't much to learn were allowed to sit at the back of the class and make decorations. But now that the play was only a week away, and his mother and father and Charlie were coming, he felt most indignant. He decided to have a word with Miss Peterson about it.

'I could learn a bit more if you like, miss,' he offered casually.

'A bit more! But Tommy, you can't even remember the lines you've got,' sighed Miss Peterson.

'Yes, well, I'll easily learn them two lines tonight. Only *now* I think it's a pretty interesting play. And I think the shepherds are pretty interesting, too. But they don't have enough to *say*; they just go around putting their arms up in the air, and kneeling, and lying down. I could easily learn a few more lines.'

This was probably the longest speech Tommy Mac had ever made to a teacher. Miss Peterson stared at him open mouthed.

Denise Davenport spoke for her. 'Hasn't he got

a cheek, miss!' she gasped. 'Just because *we've* all got lots to say, he's jealous now.'

'That will do, Denise,' interrupted Miss Peterson. She felt suddenly incredibly tired. 'Go and sit down Tommy. It's too late to change the play now.'

'Have you gone bonkers?' hissed Raff when Tommy had returned to his place.

'She's a great fat pig!'

'Who is?'

'That Denise Davenport.'

'She's not a pig—she's an angel,' giggled Raff.

Denise was standing with her small round stomach stuck out, being fitted into a white dress. She kept glancing towards Tommy, and then studiously raised her eyes to the ceiling.

'She's got loads to say,' sulked Tommy.

'So what?' said Chai. 'What do you want to talk for all of a sudden, anyway? None of *us* do. You ought to be jolly glad we've just got to stand around with sticks and sheep and things.'

'Nessy doesn't just stand around,' went on Tommy; 'he's a king, with jewels and gold boxes all over him.'

'Oh yeah, yeah, man! I'm that posh black fella,' laughed Nessy, strutting across the back of the room with a chalk box balanced on his head. 'Ah, come on Mac, wack, forget it. Let's finish this model.'

The four of them were making a model of an Eskimo council estate. A piece of broken glass, stuck down with frosted sticky tape, mirrored two cotton-wool polar bears. The igloos were made of half egg-shells, painted white, and the Eskimos were covered with real white hair which Tommy had managed to cadge from his father's barber. Normally, Tommy would have been very interested in it, but all he could think about now was the Christmas play and his small part in it. All he had to say was, 'Show us the way to this stable,' and later, 'Lo, we come bearing gifts.' And that line, he considered, sounded pretty stupid.

All that week, Denise Davenport preened and posed. She kept shouting her part aloud, in spite of being told repeatedly not to.

'Behold!' she cried. 'I bring you tidings of great joy . . . I'm having my hair permed tomorrow, miss.'

'That's good,' said Miss Peterson absently. She had decided that this was to be the last Christmas play she would ever produce.

'And me mam says she'll buy me some silver shoes. I've already got silver shoes but I've been to that many parties in them, me mam says I may as well have some new ones if I'm going to be the most important angel.'

'Get her!' gasped Chai.

The lesser angels stared dumbly at Denise, and then at their very ordinary white pumps. One, indeed, was wearing black lace-ups and was slowly working her feet round the back of the waste-paper basket.

Mr Mac was sympathetic. 'All famous actors start with small parts,' he said. 'Some even have only one line. At least you've got two.'

Tommy brightened, but only a little.

Mr Mac went on, 'And, you see, they practise and practise this one line until it's so perfect, and they *do* it so perfect that everyone notices them. Sometimes they even steal the limelight from the fellas with great long parts and become famous.'

Tommy brightened completely then, and took Count and Dracula rat hunting along the river shore. He knew he was a good actor, and he knew that he was going to steal the limelight.

The dress rehearsal, like most dress rehearsals, went off like a damp firework, and then the actual day of the play arrived. On special occasions, and this was one of them, Mrs Mac believed in sending Tommy to school really smart. She stripped him and sat him on the back kitchen draining board. A clean set of underwear hung ready on the clothes maiden. She then scrubbed his ears until he thought he'd never hear again. Unlike mothers in television advertisements, with their mild smooth soaps, she employed a pan scrubber on his knees.

Mr Mac offered some of his 'Ranger 99' for Tommy's hair. 'They won't recognise me!' complained Tommy. 'I'm supposed to be a shepherd, not a flippin' filum star!'

But Mrs Mac knew her job. She entombed him in his clean clothes and personally saw him as far as the school door. Then she hurried home to 'do' Charlie.

At two o'clock, precisely, the hall filled up with parents. Mrs Mac, dragging Charlie, bustled up to the front to bag a good spec, as she put it. Mr Mac remained at the back with a group of fathers. The stage curtains occasionally bulged out over the hall, and then Charlie could see lots of glitter, and feet, and coloured lights. There were thuds and giggles and somebody saying 'stop it'. Charlie grew bored and decided that he wanted to go and investigate the school toilets. By the time Mrs Mac had got him back the curtains were opening.

'Aaah!' cried the parents.

A group of infants in unbelievably short skirts stood ready to sing. A few of them started with the piano, the rest energetically tried to catch up. One of the smallest began to scream and was snatched swiftly into the wings.

Charlie liked that bit; he gurgled with laughter and wouldn't be silenced.

'Did you see that fairy, mam? She went wheeee into tut curtains! I wish they'd all go'n do it.' He went on tittering until the curtain fell again.

There were more thuds and giggles, and sounds of heavy props being moved around, until, at last, it was time for the main play.

Everyone liked the Christmas play, although they'd seen it every year and it was more or less the same each time. Kings and shepherds travelled backwards and forwards across the stage. Angels burst through the black star-studded curtain and floated reverently around singing carols. Charlie grunted softly against his mother's chest. Then came the scene in which Tommy said his two lines. 'Wake up, Charlie, here's our Tommy,' nudged Mrs Mac.

A loud crash brought Mr Jones hurrying from the back of the stage. The shepherds had just entered and Tommy had started the scene by tripping over the dressing gown Miss Peterson had lent him.

'There he is!' yelled Charlie. 'Hiya Tommy!'

Tommy picked himself up with dignity and had a quick look along the front row for his mother. He smiled slyly at her and then took up his position with the other shepherds.

'Tolc!' muttered Raff.

'What's a tolc?' hissed Tommy.

'A backward clot!' Raff answered through the fur of a toy dog which was supposed to be a lamb.

Tommy gently ground the end of his staff into the back of Raff's foot.

The scene dragged on. Being a good actor was not as easy as he had thought; all he was obliged to do for the moment was to kneel on one knee and pretend to warm his hands by the fire. He began to wobble. Then the back of his leg started to itch. He had never had such an itch in the whole of his life. He began to work his big toe up the back of his leg. He had no sooner reached the offending spot when the end of his nose began to itch, and then he was itching all over. It was agony. It reminded him of a time once when he'd slept with Chai at Summer Camp. It was a game they'd invented. 'Bet your arm's going to itch,' Tommy would have to say. Then Chai would have to see how long he could go without frantically scratching his arm. Then it would be his turn to bet Tommy that the soles of his feet, or his ears, were itching.

Now Tommy glanced at Chai, but Chai was

busy studying the Bethlehem sky, which is what he was supposed to be doing. Then it happened. Denise Davenport burst through the curtain, silver shoes and wings a-glistening, and in a voice more worthy of a sergeant major than an angel, shrieked, 'Fear not!'

Tommy forgot about revenge. The old urge swept over him. He really must be a good actor, he thought to himself. Now he really felt like a shepherd high up on a hillside. It was snowing, and the stars were out; thousands of them. And there was one specially big one. It surely must mean something. It hadn't been there a moment ago. More than that, there was a strange light in the sky; an *unearthly* light and with it came the strangest feeling that something unearthly was about to happen. Tommy could feel the sheep crowding round him for warmth.

'Give over, you're squashing me!' gasped Raff.

'It's hopeless,' thought Tommy. 'One can't act properly along with amateurs.' It took him some time to get back into his mood. He had just got back into it when Denise shouted again, 'I bring you tidings of great joy. Be not afraid.'

Tommy flung himself vigorously to the ground. He *was* afraid. Something unearthly *was* happening. In spite of the angel's words, he was frightened and astonished. He crawled around the hillside, hiding behind first one sheep and then another. He made a break and ran for cover behind a large rock. In the distance he could hear laughter. That struck him as odd—it wasn't in the script—but there was still the shock of actually seeing an angel to be acted out. The other shepherds weren't helping much. Come to think of it, they were just standing around looking stupid, their mouths gaping like goslings. For a second, Tommy thought he heard his name, and Mr Jones saying it. But he acted on with spirit. The angel had finished speaking and was clasping her robe tightly round her. 'Absolutely rotten acting,' thought Tommy absently.

'Jump on that box now, Tommy. She'll never catch you up there!' hooted Charlie Mac. He had never been to such a good show.

At that moment, Tommy tripped again, this time over the shepherd's fire. Logs rolled in all directions like skittles. Beneath them, for all to see, was a red light bulb supported in a milk crate. Tommy grabbed at the nearest thing he could find. It was the skirt of Denise's dress. It came away from the bodice with a sickening tearing noise.

'Oh Lor!' The tears were now streaming down Charlie's red face. 'I can see that girl's knickers!'

The audience could contain itself no longer and burst into loud guffaws of laughter. Mr Jones covered his face with his hands.

Tommy was stunned. He wondered, without much hope, if Mr Jones was laughing too. All the snow had gone. The stars had gone. And Denise had gone. She was busy having hysterics in the corridor. Mercifully the curtain dropped. It wasn't the right time for it to drop but it did so.

Tommy retreated to the safest place he knew for the five minute interval, and then swiftly rejoined the shepherds for the final act. He stood as if made of stone. He had finished with acting. If the others had co-operated with him instead of leaving him to work so hard, he wouldn't have become exhausted and fallen over the fire. He would be a driver when he grew up, same as he'd always intended to be—out on the high roads and the motorways and not stuck on some stuffy stage with a lot of made-up pansies.

The play ended. Tommy leapt from the stage and tore down to the classroom. With lightning movements he changed from his shepherd's gear into his own. The others were just leaving the stage as he charged for the side entrance. His hand was on the door knob and he had one leg through the door, when he was arrested by a thunderous voice . . .

'Tommy!'

It was Mr Jones. Tommy turned round. 'Yes, sir?' he said limply.

A tortured smile played over Mr Jones' thin lips. 'Have a good holiday, lad,' he said.

## 9. Up the Great North

One very special Friday night Mr Mac said, 'I'm taking you with me tonight, Tommy. Your mam has packed your things. I think it'll do you good to see how the other half lives. And we'll have you back in time for school on Monday.'

'You're kidding!' whooped Tommy disbelievingly.

'No, I'm not. Go and wash your face and put your boots on; it's probably cold where we're going.'

'Where *are* we going, dad?' gasped Tommy.

'I'm taking a load up to Edinburgh. Look sharp there before I have second thoughts.'

Tommy Mac shot into the back kitchen to clean up.

'Your dad's giving you a right treat, Tommy,' said Mrs Mac fondly. 'Be good and do what he tells you.'

Tommy couldn't remember going anywhere before and the thought of it made him feel quite giddy.

Outside the front door stood the big lorry. It was silver and blue, and the lights were on.

'What's in it, dad?' asked Tommy.

'Tinned stuff—all sorts,' answered Mr Mac.

'Are we going to sleep in it?' Tommy wanted to know.

'You *are* tuppence ha'penny. I've had *my* kip. You're going to curl up tight and go to sleep.'

But Tommy Mac couldn't keep his eyes shut as the big lorry moved off. For mile upon mile the streets were lit up brightly. He thought of Raff and Chai in their beds down Paradise Way and he just couldn't think about sleep. His dad, big and burly, sat beside him at the wheel, smoking a cigarette and scowling at the road. Shops and houses scudded by. Tommy could see people watching television in their front rooms and late night revellers walking home from pubs. Soon the houses grew fewer and trees and fields took their place. It was very dark now and only the headlights of the lorry lit up the countryside.

Tommy began to feel drowsy and then the last thing he remembered was being tucked into bed by his father between clean, hard sheets in a room he didn't know. He sank into the bed as if he were drowning in a huge white sea. The sea pushed him this way and that and he was glad that it was warm. Sometimes he dreamt about Paradise Way. And sometimes he dreamt about school, and Mr Jones, and crocodiles, and wrestling with Whacker Casey. Then Dracula was licking his face and he was taking him for a walk down to the iron bridge which led to one of the docks. There were roses growing all over the dock wall.

'Wake up, wake up,' a voice kept saying.

The roses grew pinker; they were spreading

across the wallpaper. Tommy's father was bending over him. 'Wake up,' he was calling.

It was a few minutes before Tommy realised that he was not in Paradise Way but in a strange roadside boarding-house. A wonderful smell of bacon was stealing up the stairs. At home, bacon was a Sunday treat only, and even then there wasn't much of it. But here, in the boarding-house, the plates were piled high, not only with bacon but with egg and sausages, too. And his father and he had a teapot and hot-water jug all to themselves.

Mr Mac was enjoying the look of excited pleasure on his son's face. 'Eat as much bread as you can lad,' he advised, 'it's all paid for.'

It was Saturday morning. Saturday morning was messages morning, and swilling out the yard morning, and the morning for standing in a longer than usual queue for fish and chips. But this particular Saturday morning had a large, delicious question mark hanging over it. All around them sat tablefuls of other lorry drivers. A lot of them seemed to know Mr Mac.

'Mornin' George,' they said, 'see you further up the Great North.'

Tommy felt proud of his father—so big and strong, his hands like enormous shovels. He wore his usual red and green checked shirt. He was like a cowboy—a cowboy of the high road. At home he didn't speak much. When he came in he was usually tired; he ate and went to bed. His life outside the house had always been a mystery to Tommy. He was just dad, who gave Mrs Mac

pound notes and gave Tommy his weekly pocket money. Tommy swaggered out after him to the road and climbed up into the lorry.

'Do you know what this road is called, lad?' asked Mr Mac. 'It's the Great North Road. It was originally built by the Romans. By gum! they knew how to build roads—straight as a die it is; no fiddling about going round corners; straight over 'em and through 'em it goes with no messing.'

Tommy was impressed. Miss Peterson didn't tell him interesting things like that.

'I bet you'd have made a better teacher than old Miss Peterson,' Tommy said. 'I bet the kids 'ud listen to *you*.'

'No fear!' laughed Mr Mac. 'I'd rather travel the roads for ten bob a week than cope with forty like you. I'd want danger money for that job; same as steeplejacking and taking unexploded bombs to pieces. I wouldn't have your teacher's job for a big clock with solid gold bells on it.'

The quiet hum of the diesel engine and the pleasant smell of it made Tommy feel pleasantly sleepy; his Dad had to concentrate, but Tommy could lean back like a lord and look out of the window. He was fascinated by the small stone villages they passed. Every house, no matter how small, had a garden. There were no chip papers flying around; no dumped prams or rubbish. The grass was greener than he thought grass could be. But the sky was a peculiar yellowish grey.

'We're going to have snow, I think, before the day's out,' observed Mr Mac.

It wasn't long coming. At first, odd flakes like feathers blew around in ones and twos. And then they began to fall more steadily. Mr Mac switched on his windscreen wipers. At the next transport café they stopped to eat. Hungrily, they wolfed down steak and chips and treacle pudding. Tommy had cream soda, and Mr Mac disappeared into the bar for a pint. When they came out of the café the snow was falling fast. It had already covered the ground.

'Oh lor!' said Mr Mac. 'It's coming down for real.'

At the next shop they came to, he jumped down for sandwiches, tea and milk.

'I hope we won't need them,' he said, 'but better to be safe than sorry.'

Tommy was full of steak and treacle pudding.

He wasn't interested in the sandwiches. He was half asleep again when Mr Mac said, 'Look out Tommy, we're coming to a big bridge. In half an hour we'll be in Scotland.'

Five minutes later they crossed a long bridge. Below was the mouth of a wide river which led straight into the sea. Tommy could see grey waves crashing against a long pier which had a yellow lighthouse at the end of it. There were small fishing boats in a harbour beneath. On the opposite bank stood an old town with a town hall clock. The roofs of the town showed red beneath the snow. Tommy would have liked to have stayed to look round, but Mr Mac was anxious to drive on. The snow was now quite thick. A sign which marked the Scottish border was practically obliterated. Mr Mac was driving cautiously and much more slowly.

'Look!' cried Tommy. 'There's a car stuck at the roadside.'

'Mmmmn,' said Mr Mac, looking worried.

They were climbing now. There were fewer houses and fewer trees. It reminded Tommy of a picture of Switzerland in the school corridor. The windscreen wipers were having trouble pushing away the snow. And then the engine started to make a strange noise. Suddenly it stopped altogether.

Mr Mac heaved on the brake. 'No good driving when I can't see,' he said.

'Where are we, Dad?' asked Tommy.

'In the middle of the Antarctic, by the look of it,' muttered Mr Mac under his breath. 'In another hour we should have been supping in The Pig and Whistle. Now, lad, we'll be lucky if we see it by morning.'

Tommy was thrilled; this was a real live adventure: stranded in the middle of nowhere with nothing but hills of snow around them.

There was a sudden soft thud behind the lorry. Mr Mac jumped out to see what was happening.

'Clivey, man!' Tommy heard his father say. 'It's real good to see you. How's this for a night out? My wheels are stuck plumb in a snow drift.'

'Well, I might as well stay with you,' Clivey answered. 'I wouldn't get more than a mile further in weather like this.'

Clivey had a red lamp which he hung on the tailboard of his lorry, and then he came round to see Tommy.

'Well now, laddy,' he said, 'how do you like this?'

'It's smashing,' Tommy said.

Clivey and Mr Mac laughed heartily. But Mr Mac was worried; he knew that in an hour or two Tommy wouldn't think it was quite so smashing.

The snow swirled softly round the lorry. It was the thickest snow Tommy had ever seen. At home when it snowed, the Corpy were out with lorries of grit and salt, and the whiteness was churned instantly to brown and then black slush. Old women grumbled at getting their boots dirty, and children used it as a heaven sent excuse for being late for school. But this was real TV newstime snow. He opened the cab door and saw that it was now halfway up the wheels.

Mr Mac was used to snow. Surprisingly, he didn't think it was pretty or exciting. He produced a primus stove and a kettle. He filled the kettle with snow and proceeded to boil it. Under the dashboard he found two hot water bottles.

'I'm hungry,' complained Tommy Mac.

'And you'll stay that way for another couple of hours,' his father promised.

'But what about those sandwiches you bought?'

'You'll get them in due course. And due course is when I say it's time to eat them.'

The cab was beginning to grow cold. Mr Mac filled one of the hot water bottles and said, 'Here, lad, put this under your jacket and cover up with this sheet.'

The sheet was a large tarpaulin. Tommy felt much better. He would have dozed off, only Mr Mac and Clivey were chatting and sharing a bottle of whisky. They gave Tommy a tiny sip and it warmed him all over . . .

Suddenly a car struggled past their lorry and drew to a halt. A young man in a tweed jacket and green kilt got out first. Then a woman followed. She was carrying a baby which was wrapped up tightly in a shawl, and she looked frightened. Mr Mac opened the cab door a few inches.

'How far are we from the nearest town?' asked the man.

'About ten miles, mate,' answered Mr Mac. 'I'm afraid you'll never make it. Best stay near us if you're wise.'

The young man explained this to his wife, trying

his best to sound cheerful. But his wife burst into tears. 'The baby's going to catch his death of cold, Hamish,' she cried.

She had a funny sort of voice, Tommy thought.

'Listen, love,' said Mr Mac, 'there's space in the back of the lorry for you and the baby; it will be warmer than your car. You can wrap this tarpaulin round you,' he said, dragging it unceremoniously from Tommy. 'And here's a hot water bottle.'

The young woman stopped crying and curled up in the back of the lorry beside the tins of fruit and salmon.

'You're tougher than that baby,' explained Mr Mac to his son, who was starting to shiver.

Tommy knew he mustn't grumble. Explorers at the South Pole didn't winge just because they were cold. He wondered what they *did* do.

'What's the capital of Italy?' asked Clivey briskly.

'Rome!' cried Tommy.

'Clever!' said Clivey. 'S'your turn.'

'How many legs has a centipede?' asked Tommy.

'Hundred, maybe?' said Mr Mac tentatively.

'Yeah, probably,' answered Tommy, who wasn't sure. 'Now it's your go, Dad.'

They played this game for a long time. The man in the kilt won. He seemed to be pretty clever. But Mr Mac and Clivey were clever in a different sort of way; both of them were equipped with food, whereas the young man was not. Tommy decided that he preferred his dad's sort of cleverness best.

Mr Mac relit the primus stove to make a cup of

tea, while Clivey trailed back to his own lorry to collect meat pies and potato crisps.

'It's stopped snowing,' he yelled, 'but it's coming over my boots.'

The young couple had nothing, so there was less food to go round, but there was plenty of hot tea for all of them. Tommy had never enjoyed a cup of tea so much in his whole life. He buried his face in the mug, and warm perspiration rolled down his nose and upper lip. The cab steamed up with warm breath and cigarette smoke. Some of the snow on the windscreen melted and slithered down in small chunks.

'Five o'clock,' said Mr Mac, 'a few hours before daylight. Then perhaps we might see a snow plough.'

Twice more, Mr Mac brewed tea and served it straight from the kettle. The baby obligingly snored and snuffled away comfortably. It behaved just as if it was still in it's centrally heated nursery. 'It's that fat on it, I suppose,' Tommy thought.

He began to sing, 'Oh, we won't go home 'til morning, we won't go 'til morning, we won't go home 'til morning . . .'

'Till daylight doth appear, till daylight doth appear (bom bom),' thundered Clivey in his deep he-man's voice.

'Oh, the burr looked over the mountain,' joined in Mr Mac.

'The *what*?' asked the young man.

'The burr.'

'Oh, you mean the bearrrr,' laughed the young man.

'Suit yourself,' said Mr Mac. 'To see what he could see,' he went on unselfconsciously.

In the end, daylight *did* appear. And with it came the snow plough. It moved through the snow like a benign monster, dividing it into two clean white cliffs on either side of the road.

'Got a shovel, man?' the driver yelled to Mr Mac.

'Yes, ta, mate,' Mr Mac yelled back.

As was his custom before tackling any job—even filling in his football coupon—Mr Mac regaled himself with tea. Then he jumped to the ground and, with the help of Clivey, shovelled away with a will. In about an hour they had freed both lorries and the car. The three vehicles

moved off slowly, skidding and shoving through the crisp snow.

At long last they reached a small town called Muirhead. Here the young man came into his own. He signalled the lorries to stop and insisted that he should treat them all to breakfast.

The Thistle and Crown was a little too posh for Mr Mac's liking. The tablecloths, unlike the tea-stained checked cloths of the transport cafés, were as white as the snow they'd just battled through. Smart waiters replaced the homely waitresses Mr Mac was used to. The menu was a couple of miles long. He felt suddenly terribly sophisticated and plumped for kedgeree. Clivey chose ham and eggs.

'If ever you're in Edinburgh,' said the young man, 'you simply must stay with us.'

'Yes indeed,' said his wife.

Clivey thanked them insincerely. But Mr Mac, still in his sophisticated mood, thought that he just might do that. They all agreed that it had been a thundering good breakfast, shook hands and parted ways.

At last Tommy and his father reached Edinburgh. Tommy thought it was a wonderful city. In the park there was a clock made entirely of flowers, and it worked too. On the hill above the city was an imposing grey castle. Mr Mac, who had been there before, showed Tommy around it.

'You know you're not going to get back in time for school, don't you?' Mr Mac reminded him.

'Ugh! I don't *never* want to go back home. I like it here; it's terrific.'

'Ah now, holidays isn't real life; you have 'em and go home happy you was that lucky.'

'Yes, sure dad,' grinned Tommy Mac.

## 10. Thieves in the Night

Tommy was bored. Whenever he was bored he went to sit outside on the front doorstep. It was a good place for thinking—or rather, for not thinking. More often than not there was more going on in the street than there was on the telly. Tonight was an exception; absolutely nothing was happening. It wasn't very warm either. Tommy scowled down Paradise Way towards the docks at the bottom of the street. It was lighting-up time and suddenly all the lights went on together: the street lights and the lights by the river. They were strangely comforting. He was beginning to feel some stirring of excitement when his mother yelled . . .

'Tommy! It's eight o'clock. Run down to McCann's and get six chips and four fish; your dad's up.'

'Yes, mam,' yelled Tommy, glad of something to do.

He met Raff and Chai in the 'chippy'. The three of them tangled in a friendly punch-up behind the door, and the bell which hung on top of it clanged like the bell on a fire engine.

'Boys!' scolded Mrs McCann. 'Do you mind

116

if I serve them and get them out?' she asked the front of the queue.

It was a trick that always worked, and the boys rolled out into the street joyfully. They punched and shoved each other until Raff dropped a piece of cod down a grid and had to go back into the shop and start all over again.

'Where's Nessy, then?' asked Tommy afterwards.

'He's gone to the stadium to watch his brother box Big Joe the Babe,' said Raff.

The boys sighed. They all envied Nessy. No one could seriously disagree with a guy whose brother was a boxer.

'Hey!' exclaimed Chai. 'The fight's on the telly, Nessy said. I'm off home to watch!'

He raced up the hill and Tommy and Raff set off for home with their fish and chips. When Tommy reached Number Seven his mother was on the step waiting for him.

'Come on,' chided Mrs Mac, 'your dad's sitting here waiting.'

Mr Mac was sitting in state at the kitchen table with his knife and fork poised ready for action. His muscles were magnificent. They rippled and bulged round the armholes of his dazzling white vest. Tommy stood and admired them.

'Come on, our Tommy,' his father said, 'what have you been doing?'

'Nothing,' answered Tommy.

'Oh, same as usual then,' said Mr Mac, starting on his fish and chips with enormous energy.

'Where are you going tonight, dad?' asked Tommy after a while.

'York,' muttered Mr Mac indistinctly.

'Can't I come with you?'

'Not this time, lad. I'm picking up one of the fellas at Manchester.' He ruffled his son's hair, took his scarf and jacket from the back of his chair and then he was gone.

Maureen and Stevey were sitting in front of the television set while the younger ones played behind the settee.

'Can I have the boxing on?' Tommy asked.

'No, you can't,' snapped Maureen. 'We're watching Johnny Race and we aren't switchin' him off just for you.'

'But you can watch the telly all night,' grumbled Tommy. 'I only want to watch the boxing. *That* fella sings like a cat with tonsillitis.'

'You cheeky little ignoramus!' gasped Maureen indignantly. 'Go to bed if you don't like it. Go on, all of you. Get upstairs to bed; you clutter up the place something awful. Go on, before Stevey and I get real mad.'

Mags and Kate went up to bed with their comics; Charlie crawled through into the back kitchen to find Mrs Mac; and Tommy slithered out into the street again.

It was spitting rain but it was the time of night that Tommy liked best. Raff had also escaped from the domestic scene.

'Attaboy, Raff,' Tommy greeted him. 'What shall we do?'

'Dunno,' said Raff.

'Oh, you always say you don't know,' complained Tommy. 'Why do I always have to think of things to do?'

'Because you always think of better things to do, that's all,' said Raff humbly. 'You wouldn't be leader of our gang if you didn't, would you?'

'I guess not,' agreed Tommy, hitching up his trousers and walking cowboy-style along the edge of the kerb. 'All right, then, I've thought. We'll have a look along the waterfront.'

The dock gates were closed. But there were ways and means of climbing over them. They managed it with nonchalant expertise.

'S'quiet, isn't it?' Raff observed.

'Well, we won't bump into our Stevey, anyway,' said Tommy. 'He's busy watching that soppy Johnny Race fellow. Him and Maureen's growing up dead stupid. Why they couldn't watch the boxing—something decent like that—I don't know.'

'Our Greta's just as daft,' Raff sympathised. 'She spends all her time messing around with her face, trying to make it look better. But you should see it when she's finished, she'd scare off Frankenstein. I bet if . . .'

'Sssh!' hissed Tommy, shoving his elbow straight into Raff's stomach. 'There's somebody in that shed. Didn't you hear that bump?'

'No,' whispered Raff. A strange tingling feeling spread up his arms and up the back of his legs.

They crept to the door of a large wooden shed. It was unlocked. Tommy opened it half an inch, and then shut it again swiftly.

'There's two fellas in there,' he said hoarsely.

'Hey, Tommy, let's go.' Raff clutched Tommy's sleeve and tried to pull him away.

'Why? Are you turning windy all of a sudden? Don't you want to see what they're up to?'

'But they might be criminals, Tommy. They ain't dockers because the lights aren't on in there.

And if they *see* us, they might get desperate and maybe even shoot us!' Raff shuddered.

'Oh, shut up, can't you!' whispered Tommy, 'or they *will* hear. Go home to your Greta if you're scared, and I'll tell Chai and Nessy that you're a skinny long chicken.'

'Don't you call me a chicken. I'm just using my brains. You've got to be careful when you're dealing with criminals. Real detectives don't just go bashing in. They use their brains first.'

But they did 'bash in'. Tommy tripped over a loose cobblestone and they both fell flat on their faces on the ground. The noise they made seemed enormously loud. They crouched behind a large wooden crate and held their breath. The door of the shed opened slowly and the beam of a torch shone over the top of the crate.

'Did you 'ear summat, Fred?' one of the men whispered.

'Yeah, it came from over there by t'crate.'

Tommy was scared. He could hear Raff's heart beating like an African tom-tom and he scowled threateningly at him through the darkness. Suddenly, there was a scuffling sound just outside the shed, and a tin clattered over the ground.

'Huh!' laughed Fred. 'It was only a ginger moggy!'

'A ginger what?' asked the other.

'A ginger cat. I fort it was a perishin' rozzer. Bless me, you don't half get some frights on this job!'

They went back into the shed, leaving the door ajar. Tommy and Raff peered over the top of the crate. They could see the men inside the shed now. One of them was prising open a packing case while the other held the torch. The boys ducked down behind the crate again.

'What do you think they're pinching?' breathed Raff.

'Dunno for sure,' whispered Tommy, 'but those packets they're taking out of that packing case look jolly like cigarettes.'

'Crumbs!' gasped Raff. 'There must be hundreds of fags there.'

'*Thousands* more like,' said Tommy.

'Well, what do you think we ought to do?' Raff asked. He felt less like a skinny long chicken now and more like a special agent.

'They've broken the padlock on the shed door,' said Tommy. 'If we can find a thinnish piece of metal we could wedge it into the catch and that would hold them prisoner. For a little while, anyway.'

They searched around feverishly, and then Tommy found a length of broken railing.

'It was lying around waiting for us!' he whispered.

Surprised by his own bravery, Tommy crept up to the shed and quietly pushed the door closed. Then he wedged the piece of metal into the door catch. The men were still intent on their work inside and didn't seem to notice that the door was now shut. The boys crept quickly back to the dock gate and swarmed over it into the street.

'What are we going to do now, Tommy?' panted Raff.

'Call the police, of course, and then we can sit and watch the fun.'

The first telephone kiosk they found was out of order; in fact, the telephone was missing altogether. They raced down Fish Street to another which proved to be in working order. Tommy dialled 999.

'Police, please!' he shouted when the operator answered. Then, 'Hullo, is that the police? Well, we've just locked two thieves in Melvin Dock.'

'Who has?' asked a suspicious voice.

'We has—have,' said Tommy.

'Sounds like a kid. Are you having me on?' asked the voice.

'No, of course I'm not having you on.' Tommy was getting angry. 'Aren't you even going to come and see? If you don't come quickly they'll get away and then maybe they'll come and catch us and give us a good clobbering, and then you'll be sorry only it'll be too late then.'

'All right, all right,' said the voice, 'there's nothing much doing at this end so we may as well pop over. What's your name, lad?'

'Tommy Mac from Paradise Way.'

'Oh *you!*' said the voice. 'Well, I know exactly where to come if this turns out to be a joke.'

'Oh come *on!*' yelled Tommy, exasperated.

'We're coming now,' said the voice.

Tommy replaced the receiver and joined Raff in the street. 'We'll go back and see what happens,' he said.

Both boys now felt decidedly safer. They ran back to the dock gate and, for the second time that night, climbed into the yard. From the direction of the shed they could hear muffled, angry voices. When the men started to hammer at the door, Tommy said, 'Gosh! They're going to get out of there before the police arrive.'

There was a sound of splintering wood, and Tommy and Raff decided that it was really time to go. But, just at that moment, the dock gates swung open and two police cars and a blue van shot into the yard, their blue lights flashing. The doors of the van opened and out leapt two policemen and two dogs. The silence was shattered by cries and barks and shouts, and the blue lights of the cars twirled round and round and stabbed the darkness with colour.

'I told you it'd be smashing!' exclaimed Tommy. 'Just listen to that din!'

He jumped onto a bin; his face was red with excitement.

'I think I'll be a rozzer when I grow up,' declared Raff admiringly. 'All those smashing buttons and helmets and things; and cars that you can go as fast as you like in; and sirens and things on them. I think it'd be better than being a cowboy.'

'You couldn't have been a cowboy in England, anyway,' observed Tommy.

'I could've gone to America, couldn't I? And bought myself a horse and a gun as soon as I got there? But it saves a lot of bother just to stay here and be a policeman.'

'Huh! I bet you'll just end up selling bacon and stuff behind a counter after all the things you've

said you're going to be. I bet you'll have forgot all about joining the police by the time you're grown up,' scoffed Tommy.

'No, I won't!' yelled Raff and pushed Tommy off the bin.

'Right! You've asked for it!' cried Tommy Mac, leaping up from the ground, his fists at the ready.

He was interrupted by the police clattering back through the yard with the dogs pulling at their leashes and barking furiously. With them, hand-cuffed and miserable, were Fred and his mate.

'Hey, look, Raff, there's Constable Jackson,' shouted Tommy.

Constable Jackson flashed his torch on to the two boys. 'Well, well,' he said. 'Look who's here. You weren't having us on after all, were you?'

'I told you the truth, didn't I?' said Tommy proudly.

'So you did. But don't forget, you've told me quite a lot of hair-raising tales off and on, haven't you?'

'S'pose I have,' grinned Tommy.

'However, tonight's job deserves a lift home. Come on, lads, hop in.'

It was the second time that Tommy had ridden in Constable Jackson's police car but it was a treat all the same. The constable even shook hands with him when they arrived outside Number Seven, Paradise Way.

'Where on earth have you been?' asked his mother when Tommy rushed joyfully into the kitchen.

'Just out, Mam.'

'I can *see* that! You're black with dirt.'

When he had washed and was ready for bed, Tommy couldn't resist telling his mother all about the thieves and the police cars.

'You'll get yourself into serious trouble one of these days, our Tommy,' said Mrs Mac disapprovingly. Then, suddenly, she gave him a massive and unexpected hug. 'Now, off upstairs to bed with you.'

## 11. Charlie is Temporarily Mislaid

In the middle of August, Mr Mac came up with a stunning surprise: he was taking the entire family to the seaside. Only Stevey, who had to work, was to stay behind. Occasionally, Mrs Mac mustered up the energy to take the children 'over the water' for the day. But this was to be not just for the day but for a whole week; they would sleep and eat in a boarding house.

Tommy could hardly believe it. As a rule, a trip to the seaside inevitably ended in a tortuous journey home, with Mags crying, Kate feeling sick, and Charlie wanting to visit the toilet at the precise moment the bus arrived. To *live* at the seaside was a luxury that Tommy found difficult to imagine.

For Mrs Mac, the prospect of a week's holiday meant an immense amount of washing and ironing. She dared anyone to remove any of the ironed clothes from the suitcase.

'You can do with what you've got on,' she said.

The great day arrived at last, as all great days eventually do. Mr Mac, wearing a white open-necked shirt and a maroon sleeveless pullover, ordered a taxi. There were so many of them that it would work out as cheap as the bus, he argued.

Raff, Chai and Nessy stood on the corner of the street and watched enviously as Tommy and his family drove off in style towards the station.

On the train Mr Mac was in a great mood. He sang and chatted, and bought cartons of orange juice for everyone. Even Mrs Mac didn't scold; she knew that it was impossible for five children to travel for two hours on a train without getting grubby. She watched Charlie fondly as he grew grubbier and grubbier and stickier and stickier. At the last moment she produced an enormous wash-bag, full of damp sponges and useful pieces of old towelling, and cleaned him up as best she could.

The boarding house, which was called 'Seaview', really *did* overlook the sea. Tommy felt that if he grew any more excited something dangerous would happen inside; his chest was already aching. The landlady was called Mrs Miller. She showed them to their rooms and pointed out the bathroom. Both the bath and the toilet were pink, and the walls were covered with shiny tiles from floor to ceiling.

'Isn't this posh, mam?' whispered Tommy.

'Ssssh,' answered Mrs Mac, also somewhat awed. 'It's ignorant to pass remarks. Still, it *is* very nice,' she added.

For lunch they had smoked haddock and chips which smelt of the seaside. There was jam sponge to follow, and then coffee.

'Is the coffee extra?' whispered Mrs Mac anxiously to her husband.

'No, love,' interrupted Mrs Miller, who had overheard her. 'It's all in.'

Mrs Mac ordered coffee for seven. But, for her, the biggest thrill of all was to get up from the table and leave the dirty dishes; she could hardly rid herself of a feeling of guilt.

'It's your treat, Mam,' said Mr Mac, taking her arm fondly. 'Put your hat on and we'll take the kids out for buckets and spades.'

The front was choked with souvenir shops, each more gaudy than the next. Even their fancy blinds were festooned with bric-a-brac. Bunches of gaily coloured buckets and spades were strung together on the pavements and rubber snakes and spiders leered through the windows.

'I want, I want,' cried Charlie non-stop.

'Well,' said Mr Mac, 'I'm going to give each of you twenty-five pence pocket money a day, and when it's gone it's gone, and that's that.'

Even Maureen bought a bucket and spade. They all had money left over for an ice cream on the beach and then they settled down to the serious job of building a sandcastle.

Mr Mac treated his wife and himself to a couple of deckchairs and then promptly fell asleep with a knotted handkerchief covering his head. Mrs Mac blinked happily at the blue sky. The sea, from where she was sitting, was hidden from view by several hundred holidaymakers, but she didn't mind. An assortment of smells assailed her nostrils: the smells of vinegar and chips, candyfloss and seaweed.

'What's that horrible smell?' complained Charlie.

'It's seaweed, love,' explained Mrs Mac, laughing. 'Don't you like it?'

'No, I don't,' he said; 'it stinks!'

'It's a super smell!' exclaimed Tommy joyfully. 'I could go on smelling it for ever and ever.'

At that moment, a somewhat ancient donkey came plodding past. Mrs Mac gave her sleeping husband a sly look.

'Here you are, Tommy,' she whispered, slipping some coins into his hand, 'take your brother on the donkeys.'

Tommy grabbed Charlie's fat little hand and dragged him off to the starting post. Charlie liked the donkeys. He wobbled along contentedly. But

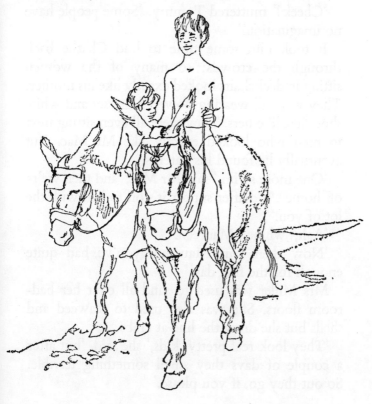

Tommy was far away from the crowded beach—
he was crossing a parched Mexican desert. Brigands
were lying in wait to capture him. Charlie, riding
beside him, was his second-in-command. The sun
beat down unmercifully on his head. There were
miles and miles of uncharted desert to cross. Each
ice cream cart was an abandoned wagon. His men
depended on Tommy winning through to civilisa-
tion and he was most indignant, therefore, when
the girl who was leading his pony said, 'All right,
then, that's your lot!' and unceremoniously pushed
him off.

'Cheek!' muttered Tommy. 'Some people have
no imagination.'

It took him some time to lead Charlie back
through the crowds; so many of the women
sitting in deckchairs looked exactly like his mother.
They were all wearing flowered dresses and white
shoes just like hers. They were all even sitting next
to men who looked exactly like Mr Mac. But
eventually he found his parents.

'One more swim,' said Mr Mac, 'and then we're
off home. And after supper it's off to bed with the
lot of you.'

'Aah,' whined Maureen.

'Now then, our Maureen, you've had quite
enough for the first day.'

Mrs Miller was used to sand all over her bedroom floors. She was also used to seaweed and
shells but she drew the line at crabs.

'They look real pretty, kids,' she said, 'but after
a couple of days they smell something terrible.
So out they go, if you please.'

Reluctantly, Charlie emptied his bucketful of pink and black crabs behind a rhododendron bush in the front garden.

'Good lad,' said Mrs Miller. 'They would have smelt something terrible, I'm telling you.'

Charlie looked unbelieving.

'I've got liver and sausage and pink jellies for your suppers,' she continued, 'so come along and then you can get yourselves off to bed and give your poor mum and dad a bit of peace.'

After the liver and sausage, Tommy, who was sharing a bed with Charlie, wriggled down between the sheets and promptly fell asleep. His dad went 'up the pier' for a nightcap, and Mrs Mac sat in state in the lounge and read the glossy magazines which were arranged in fan shapes on numerous small tables.

During the past few weeks Mr Mac had worked a good deal of overtime. He had determined that Mrs Mac and the children should have a 'thumping good holiday'—as he put it—and so the following night he allowed the children to stay up late to go to the fairground.

The fair was ablaze with colour. The Big Dipper shone against the dark sky like a giant snake. Delighted screams tore the night air as the coaches rocketed towards the ground.

'Catch me on one of those!' shuddered Mrs Mac, who preferred the safety of the one-armed bandits.

Tommy had found a machine which was faulty; it coughed up pennies like an old man with bronchitis. He filled his pockets until an observant attendant moved him along. Mags and Kate had bagged two high stools at a snack bar and were in the middle of their third knickerbocker glory. Charlie was only interested in the Dodgem Cars. He rode on them for the whole evening, keeping to car number six. It was, therefore, with some concern that, at the end of the evening, Mr Mac could not find his son in car number six or in any other.

'Charlie! Charlie boy!' he called. 'Time to go home.'

But Charlie was nowhere to be found. Mrs Mac, pretending to be calm but not really calm at all, rushed round the sideshows calling, 'Charlie! Charlie! Time to go home!'

But they couldn't find him. The more the family searched, the more Charlie wasn't there.

'He's lost, he's lost!' wept Mrs Mac at last. 'My poor little Charlie, he's lost.'

'Don't be daft, Mam,' said Mr Mac, 'he's somewhere around. We'll split up and look for him and meet by the gate in half an hour.'

Tommy, who spent his days fighting Charlie, now had a nasty pain in the middle of his stomach. Perhaps Charlie had wandered out of the fairground and down to the sea. And perhaps at this very moment he was drowning. Unobserved, Tommy began to cry.

'Charlie, Charlie!' he called. 'Where are you?'

He couldn't resist the temptation to leave the fairground to look for Charlie by the sea.

It was dark on the beach and quite deserted. The deckchairs were strapped in piles and covered with tarpaulins which made sharp cracking noises in the warm breeze. The thought of Charlie lost in this eerie place made Tommy feel quite sick.

Suddenly, he saw a man coming along the shingle, being pulled along by a massive dog.

'Wotcher, matey!' the man said. 'Where's your muvver this time of night?'

Tommy was glad to meet somebody. 'I've lost my brother,' he replied.

'Lorst him?' cried the young man cheerfully. 'People don't go round losing bruvvers at the seaside these days, not in the twentieth century. It's not as easy as that. How old is this cock sparrer?'

'Four,' said Tommy.

'Four! That's even harder. I used to try to lose *my* bruvver when he was four but I never could manage it. He used to turn up every time like a bad penny. He's still doing it, and now he's *twenty*-four.'

It was impossible to stay depressed in the company of this breezy young stranger. The big dog leapt up and put his paws on Tommy's shoulders. He licked Tommy's face and wagged his tail joyfully.

'Care for a hot drink?' asked the young man briskly. 'I've nothing much to do tonight; we could talk about how to find your bruvver over a mug of something.'

The stools where Mags and Kate had been sitting were empty now. The stranger sat down and the giant hound flopped under his legs and began to snore. A blonde lady in a pink, lacy jumper served them. She gave Tommy a biscuit for nothing and the young man a wink—also for nothing.

'By the way, my name's Dinger—on account of my surname being Bell,' said the stranger. 'What's yours?'

'Tommy Mac,' said Tommy.

'A stick of that pink rock for Tommy here,' Dinger said to the blonde lady who seemed to have taken quite a fancy to Dinger's few square inches of counter. 'And another one for Charlie,' he added.

Tommy remembered Charlie, and the hot drink didn't seem as good.

'D'you know,' said Dinger, 'I must be soft in the head not to have thought about it before— you're sitting over the best detective in the world.'

Tommy looked down. 'The dog, you mean?'

'Very same. If you could lay your hands on anything belonging to your bruvver, Samson would track him down straight off.'

'But I have!' cried Tommy. 'I've got his hat right here in my pocket.' He produced a crumpled cap inscribed with the words 'Kiss Me Quick'.

'Wake up, Samson,' commanded Dinger, touching the sleeping dog with his shoe.

Samson flopped over on to his back, stretched his four paws in the air, rolled his eyes sleepily and then stood up and shook himself vigorously.

'Smell that,' commanded Dinger, thrusting the cap under the dog's nose. 'Now think about it, boy, think about it.'

Samson thought about it and then he loped off across the fairground with his nose close to the ground and his ears pointing upwards. The dog made straight for the Dodgem Cars. He spent a considerable time sniffing at car number six, which annoyed the courting couple who happened to be in it. Then he hurried off towards the main gates. Dinger and Tommy had to run to keep up with him. Samson was now running along the sea-front.

'Are you sure he knows where he's going?' asked Tommy.

'Definuly does,' panted Dinger. 'Save your bref or we'll lose him.'

Suddenly Samson stopped with a jerk. A large black building loomed up in front of them. Over the door hung a blue lamp.

'How do you like that!' laughed Dinger. 'It's the police station!'

Inside, a sleepy young policeman was propping up the counter.

'Have you got anyone here called Charlie Mac?' gasped Tommy hopefully.

'Your property?' the policeman asked.

'Yes; sir, he's my brother. We've lost him.'

'Well, maybe you've just found him,' said the yawning policeman. 'Come on.'

He led the way to the police canteen. There sat Charlie, surrounded by smiling policewomen and joyfully tucking into fish and chips. Tommy no longer felt like crying; he felt quite normal again. He grabbed his brother and started to thump him good and hard.

'Lay off, our Tommy!' screamed Charlie. 'You know what Mam said. She said if you get lost, any of you, ask a policeman, so I did.'

Tommy was infuriated but he knew this was

true. 'We've all . . . I mean, Mam and Dad have been dead worried about you.'

'D'you want a chip?' asked Charlie.

'Yes,' said Tommy, beginning to enjoy himself.

'He's a right turn, your Charlie,' giggled one of the policewomen. 'I bet he keeps your mother going.'

'*We'd* better be going,' said Tommy. 'My mam will be getting really fussed.'

At the gate of the fairground stood Mr and Mrs Mac and the others. At the sight of Charlie, Mrs Mac burst into a torrent of abuse. It was difficult to tell whether anger or relief reigned uppermost in her mind.

'I only did what you kep' saying, Mam,' said Charlie indignantly. 'You said if we got lost we had to ask a policeman.'

This was exactly what Mrs Mac *had* told them umpteen times. She didn't know whether to wallop Charlie or to hug him. Instead, she took him home and tucked him into bed.

Mr Mac, who had taken an instant liking to Dinger, went with him for a final drink. In fact, he went 'up the pier' with Dinger every night for the rest of the holiday. And nobody worried about Charlie any more because every time he got lost—which was often—Samson always found him with expert ease.

## 12. Some Have It and Some Don't

Paradise Way wasn't the place it used to be, Mrs Mac reckoned. Once it had been safe to shove the kids out into the street and not be worried. But nowadays it was crowded with traffic from one end to the other. Mr Mac himself parked a lorry most nights just outside the door, sometimes a giant one that stretched the length of the house next door as well. Lorries and vans rolled down to the dock front and back again at speeds well above the limit. And although half the people in the street couldn't manage to pay their rent, most of them seemed to be able to afford transport of one kind or another. It simply wasn't a safe street to play in any more.

Charlie Mac was laid out on the living room couch with a swollen eye and a scratched nose—results of an unsuccessful fight with a bicycle.

'Poor little love,' sighed Mrs Mac, 'he was only playing football.'

'Well, Mam,' said Mr Mac, 'the street is no place to be playing football. He should go to the park.'

'It's a bus ride to the park,' complained Mrs Mac. '*We* used to play in the middle of the street all day long and we didn't get maimed by traffic.'

'It's no good talking about them days,' said Mr Mac. 'They're gone forever.'

'Well, it's a shame, that's all,' Mrs Mac said feebly as she started on the washing up. 'D'you remember that programme on the telly a bit ago?' she continued; 'the one where those mothers marched up and down across the street with prams so that no traffic could get past?'

'I'm not having *you* make a show of yourself,' said Mr Mac firmly.

'Well, there should be *some* safe place for the likes of our Charlie to play,' said Mrs Mac.

At that moment, Tommy came tumbling into the kitchen in search of food. 'There's the 'bomby' on the corner,' he said.

'There you are!' exclaimed his father. 'There's the bomb-site.'

'But there ain't nothing there,' Tommy said. 'There ain't nothing interesting there.'

Mr Mac became suddenly thoughtful. On his travels he had seen bomb-sites which had been converted into useful places—adventure playgrounds, they were called. Looking at Charlie, his battle-scarred youngest, he suddenly agreed that things were not as they should be.

'I tell you what,' he announced importantly, 'I'll write a letter to the Corpy and ask them about it.'

As soon as he had finished his supper, he sat down and laboriously wrote the letter. Then he set off to drive to Cardiff, and dropped the letter into the first postbox he passed.

A whole week elapsed before a reply came

through the letter box of Number Seven, Paradise Way. The reply was worded in such a manner that neither Mr Mac nor his wife could properly understand it, except for a bit at the end which clearly said that the 'bomby' on the corner could *not* be made into an adventure playground. Mr Mac, who had not up until now been seriously interested in the idea, was absolutely furious.

'Who does he think he is?' he raged. 'Who does this fellow Bennett think he is?'

Tommy Mac liked his father when he was in a rage. He sounded strong and important.

'I tell you what,' Mrs Mac was saying, 'there's Mrs O'Keefe's student up the street—in Welfare or something, he is—maybe he'd go and talk for us.'

Mrs O'Keefe's student, whose name was Jim, was greatly flattered by Mr Mac's visit. He at once got on a bus and went down to see Mr Bennett, but with no success at all.

Tommy Mac was incensed when he heard this. 'It jolly well isn't fair,' he said to the gang; 'our poor Charlie only wants to play footy, and he gets all done up by a perishin' bike.'

'He should've looked out for himself,' criticised Raff sternly.

'But he's only little,' said Tommy. 'My dad's right, they should make the 'bomby' into a 'venture playground. Then Charlie could play footy without getting killed.'

'Then why don't your dad *do* something about it then?'

'He has done, only he wouldn't listen to him.'

'Who wouldn't?'

'This geezer called Mr Bennett,' said Tommy.

'A Corpy fella, is he?' asked Raff.

'I think he is,' Tommy said. 'Mrs O'Keefe's student even went down to see him but old Bennett said he couldn't do anything.'

'But he's got to do something.'

'Oh, don't talk daft!' snapped Tommy irritably. 'What are we going to do? We can't *make* him do anything if he don't want to.'

'Yes, we can,' argued Raff. 'We can go on a protest march, same as them nutty students do.'

Tommy Mac gazed at his friend in admiration. That was *exactly* what they should do. He wished he'd thought of it himself, but he said generously, 'Under that tatty red hair you've got a brain, wack. That's a jolly good idea.'

Raff shrugged. 'Where shall we protest, though?' he asked.

'Outside his house'd be a good place,' answered Tommy. 'We'll look him up in the phone book.'

The gang squeezed itself into a telephone kiosk. There was a yawning gap where the telephone should have been.

'Good job we only need the book,' commented Chai.

'D'you know his initial?' asked Raff, running a grimy finger down the Bennetts.

'Yes, it's K, I remember that,' Tommy said.

'Here it is . . . The Elms, Broadway, Seaport.'

'Oh, lahdy dah!' exclaimed Tommy Mac. 'Too posh to have a street number same as ordinary folks.'

The boys ran back to Tommy's house to collect forty pence for bus fares.

'Can I come, Tommy?' wailed Charlie, who was now covered more or less from head to foot with sticking plaster.

'No, you can't,' said Tommy.

'Ah, let him,' put in Raff. 'It *is* about him, after all.'

'Oh, all right, then,' said Tommy grudgingly.

So they took Charlie, dirty face and all, not noticing that he was still in his bedroom slippers and pyjama jacket.

It was quite a long way out to Seaport, and forty pence wasn't really enough for the bus fare. But, as luck would have it, the conductor was fed up and not in the mood for arguing. Tommy, Charlie and the gang spilled out onto the pavement at Seaport and made their way to Broadway.

'Isn't it quiet?' remarked Nessy.

'What are we whispering for?' asked Chai.

So they began to shout as they wandered past the large, dignified houses.

'Here it is!' exclaimed Tommy at last. 'The Elms.'

There wasn't a single elm tree in sight. The boys peered through a hedge into a spacious garden.

'Take a look at that!' gasped Tommy.

'S'like a bloomin' public park!' whistled Nessy.

A small fair-haired boy in blue trunks was crawling up a fibre-glass slide which sloped down to a brilliant blue swimming pool. A boy made of stone, wearing nothing at all, was emptying a vase of water into the pool in which two girls were swimming lazily.

'Fiona! Lisa! I'm coming down!' called the boy in the blue trunks.

'Whew! Listen to his voice!' choked Nessy. 'He sounds a right bit of dripping!'

'He can't half swim, though, you gotta admit that,' said Tommy Mac.

'If I had a swimming pool in our back yard I bet I could swim like that, too,' Chai snorted.

Charlie said nothing. He was too busy getting rid of his slippers and pyjama jacket. He hung them on a branch and was well on his way to the pool before the gang noticed his disappearance.

'Hey, gosh, look at your brother!' gasped Raff.

'Good heavens! Look at that little boy!' cried Fiona Bennett.

Charlie hurled himself straight into the pool and sank immediately to the bottom. It was a mistake; he'd meant to go in at the shallow end.

'Quickly!' shrieked Fiona; 'he'll drown!'

She and Lisa dived under and caught hold of Charlie by his trousers.

'You've no right to be here,' scolded the boy when Charlie had been rescued; 'this is a private pool.'

'Oh, let him stay, Justin,' said Lisa. 'Don't be mean. He's rather sweet.'

By now Charlie was a great deal cleaner.

'Gosh!' exclaimed Justin. 'There are more of them over there!'

There was not much point now in propping up

the hedge. Tommy and the gang advanced across the velvet lawns of The Elms.

'Explain yourselves,' commanded Justin. Although he wasn't very big, he had a special way of speaking. It almost put Tommy Mac off, but he said, 'We've come here to protest.'

'Really? About what?' asked Justin haughtily.

Tommy Mac started to explain. With one eye on the stone boy who was still busily filling the pool, and the other on the weedless flower beds, he described Paradise Way, and the traffic problem, and the bomb-site which Justin's father was refusing to turn into an adventure playground. The loudest noise to interrupt his long and passionate speech was the buzzing of bees among the hollyhocks.

The three Bennett children listened in silence. Then Fiona exploded hotly, 'I think that's awfully mean! Daddy should have listened to you.'

'I daresay my father had his reasons,' her brother said.

But his sisters turned on him. 'You're an old fishy face!' shouted Fiona.

'You're horrid and mean . . .' Lisa began.

'Oh, all right,' Justin interrupted. 'How do we do this protest thing of yours?'

'I dunno,' admitted Tommy. 'We've never actually done one before.'

'I guess we just make a lot of fuss and noise,' said Raff.

So that was what they decided to do.

Inside The Elms, Mrs Bennett was entertaining friends. They were playing bridge in the drawing room. The four women studied their cards, grim-lipped and silent.

'Two spades,' said Mrs Bennett at last.

'Two what?' asked one of her friends, adjusting her hearing aid.

Mrs Bennett sighed. 'I said . . .'

But she was interrupted by a deafening noise from the garden.

'We want an adventure playground!' shrilled half a dozen voices.

'Safety for kids!'

'Keep death off Paradise Way!'

Bewildered, Mrs Bennett and her friends struggled out of their chairs and made for the terrace.

'Children!' cried Mrs Bennett. '*What* are you doing?'

'Protesting,' said Justin.

'We're terribly cross with daddy,' yelled Fiona. 'He won't make the . . .'

'Bomby,' said Tommy.

'. . . the 'bomby' into an adventure playground for these boys.'

'You're standing on a begonia!' cried Mrs Bennett.

Chai moved his foot away from the crushed flower.

'Down with city planners!' bellowed Justin.

The gang looked at him admiringly.

'March round the greenhouse and back through the orchard,' laughed Lisa happily.

But, before they could, Mr Bennett clicked through the wrought-iron gate. Although the day was very hot he was entombed in striped trousers and a bowler hat and, despite the fact that a downpour would have been a meteorological miracle, he was clutching a rolled umbrella. He stopped aghast at the scene in front of him.

'Darling!' his wife greeted him hysterically. 'I'm so glad you're home.'

Tommy and his gang increased the volume of their protest.

'Corpy guys are corpses!' they yelled.

'Stop!' bellowed Mr Bennett. 'Who *are* these children?'

There was a sudden silence and then Tommy walked up to Mr Bennett and introduced himself.

'My dad wrote a letter to you,' he said accusingly, 'and I bet you never even read it.'

He went on to explain the entire situation. Mr Bennett said nothing.

'Daddy,' wheedled Lisa, 'it's not really fair, is it?' She jumped up into his arms. 'It's not at all fair, is it?'

'Hmmn, I'll think about it,' Mr Bennett mumbled.

'Oh look!' exclaimed his wife. 'There's a little one in the pool.'

'Come out, Charlie,' bellowed Tommy.

Charlie came obediently. The rubber duck he'd been playing with had sprung a leak and now lay dead and flat on the bottom.

'My dear child,' said Mrs Bennett, staring at Charlie's trousers, 'you're soaking wet.'

'Bin in the water,' explained Charlie.

'I'll find you some dry clothes,' she said. 'You can keep them.'

'No thank you, missus,' said Tommy, 'my mam'll post them on.'

Mrs Bennett studied Tommy Mac's face, started to say something, and then changed her mind.

The gang sang jubilantly all the way home.

A few days later a gang of workmen and a cement mixer appeared on the Paradise Way 'bomby'.

'What are you going to do?' Tommy asked the men.

'Lord knows!' sighed a young skiver. 'Build a load of old rubbish, I guess.'

148

The gang watched with interest for several hours as the workmen cleared the waste ground, dug trenches and erected weird shapes in concrete.

Later the same week, a group of students, including Mrs O'Keefe's, took charge. They had volunteered to help.

'Would *you* play there?' Raff asked Tommy as they stood looking at the almost completed playground.

'Well, I dunno. Our Charlie'll like it,' Tommy answered.

Mrs O'Keefe's student wandered over to them. 'Want to help get some planks from the demolition site, and some tools?' he asked.

The gang brightened. 'Yes,' said Tommy, 'that'd be great. We could build a den.'

'Or a galleon,' said Raff.

'Or a prisoner-of-war camp,' laughed Nessy.

Mr Bennett, beaten but determined not to show it, officially opened the new playground two weeks later. And Justin and his sisters were among the first to sail in Raff's galleon.

## 13. The Finding Club

The best of the hot weather had gone and so had all the holiday. With a sinking heart and wearing unfamiliar clothes Tommy trudged once more in the direction of school.

Equally unwillingly, Mr Jones opened his office and sat down at his newly polished desk. The suffocating smell of polish was, in fact, noticeable throughout the whole school. It was evident that a great many hands had spent a great many hours transforming the premises.

A stack of brand new registers lay in front of Mr Jones. They contained a host of new names: new boys and girls to be 'broken in'. There were changes on the staff, too. Miss Peterson had been suddenly called away—to the Canary Islands or somewhere equally unlikely. And there was a new teacher for 3B.

At Assembly, Mr Jones was somewhat startled to see Tommy Mac among the rank and file; it was only five to nine. He wondered—not too hopefully—if this was a good omen. He began to say 'good morning' and 'welcome back', and then he noticed a distinct lack of attention among the children; they had all turned their heads towards the back of the hall. Mr Jones followed their gaze. In the doorway stood Miss Bloom, the new teacher for 3B.

She wore a very brief bright red skirt. Her long blonde hair completely obliterated one eye and fell down to her waist. The eye that was visible was bright blue and twinkled. Around her neck hung a thick gold chain.

'Gosh!' whispered Tommy Mac softly. 'Golly!'

'Blimey!' echoed Raff.

'D'you think she's ours?' whispered Chai.

'Must be,' hissed Tommy, 'there's a fella in Miss Peterson's class.'

'Blimey!' said Raff again.

With some difficulty, Mr Jones finished the Assembly and dismissed the children.

Tommy Mac and his gang had just bagged their favourite 'spec'—the window side on the back row—when Miss Bloom entered the classroom. She ignored the chair and swung herself neatly on to the top of the desk, crossing her legs and tossing back her hair in the same movement. She surveyed the class in silence, scowling and counting to herself. The children sat—as was the custom with a new teacher—with one finger across their mouths; waiting and wondering.

In the middle of the front row sat Denise Davenport. The warm weather had done something to her hair: her ringlets were twice as thick and twice as long. A crisp lemon bow perched on top of them like a mammoth butterfly. 'Pudding face!' thought Tommy maliciously. Denise was whispering to the girl next to her.

'Stand up, that girl!' snapped Miss Bloom.

Denise rose with a pale smile.

'How *dare* you talk without leave. You're a cheeky article, and you can stand out during games.'

Denise, white with shock at being spoken to in such unfamiliar terms, burst into loud sobs.

'And stop that ridiculous racket,' added Miss Bloom. 'You're a spoilt child as well, I see.'

Tommy Mac and his gang were speechless with delight. They themselves did not expect to escape Miss Bloom's tongue but it was evident that there were going to be fair do's for all.

After Arithmetic Miss Bloom changed her shoes and led them out into the playground for rounders. Mr Jones, watching from his window, noted with astonishment that none of the children spoke in line. He cast Miss Bloom a look of grateful admiration.

With low cunning, Miss Bloom split the gang into opposing teams, and appointed Tommy bowler and herself first in to bat. Tommy, unable to resist showing off, bowled her a hard, fast ball. Miss Bloom drew back her arm and hit the ball over the playground wall and out into the street.

'Cor!' cried the class in admiration.

'That'll do,' admonished Miss Bloom. 'Behave while I go and get it.'

She had further to go than she anticipated. The street was on a hill and she had to run past two tenement blocks and then fight for the ball with a dog who was convinced that she had come especially to play with him. She returned to the playground hot and flustered. But the class was quiet; Tommy had seen to that.

'She'll have us inside if she catches us messing,' he had warned the others.

The rest of the game was very exciting. Miss Bloom would stand no cheating. This was a novel idea. With Miss Peterson—who had never really known the rules anyway—the children had been used to taking outrageous short cuts in front of the bays with the result that the score at the end of the game would be 65–60. At the end of Miss Bloom's game the score was only 10–5 but it was a glorious and well earned ten and nobody complained.

At lunchtime Tommy rushed home to tell his mother about the fabulous new teacher.

'Mam!' he called.

'Shut up, she's in bed,' answered Maureen testily. 'I'm doing your dinner.'

'Oh no!' groaned Tommy. 'We'll be dying of the stomach ache.'

'That's right,' scoffed Maureen, 'don't bother to ask about Mam.'

'What *is* wrong with her, then?' asked Tommy, beginning to feel upset.

'Haven't the faintest.' Maureen was upset herself.

'Oh, Maureen, you aren't half soppy!' Tommy exploded. 'Well, I'm going up to see her.'

'You're not,' snapped Maureen. 'She's asleep. Let her be.'

'But I've got something to tell her,' persisted Tommy.

Maureen cuffed him behind the ear with one hand and tossed an indiscriminate amount of salt into the potato pan with the other. 'Well, you can hang on to your breathtaking bit of rotten news till tea-time. Now set the table, you lazy great lump of bread puddin'.' Maureen was always bad tempered whenever she was called upon to do any extra work.

Charlie began to winge, 'Maw, maw, when's the dinner ready? My tummick's making awfully rude noises.'

'That's because it's so fat,' said Maureen; 'it'd make a better drum than a stomach.'

'You're a pig! You're a hobbible pig!' wailed Charlie. 'I'm going to tell our Mam on you if she gets better.'

'*If*?' asked Tommy, who was very worried now.

'Go and feed the dogs, you,' cried Maureen, infuriated.

'Feed the dogs?' Tommy looked at her stupidly.

'That's what I said, cloth ears—the D-O-G-S. Honestly! If our Mam didn't feed those two brutes of yours, I swear they'd drop down dead in the yard out there.'

Tommy struggled inexpertly with the tin opener, gave up and finally opened the tin of dog food with Stevey's hammer and chisel. It was comparatively peaceful in the yard with Count and Dracula. The two dogs seemed to sense that all was not well, and they were a lot more sympathetic than Maureen. Count drooped his tail between his legs and regarded Tommy with a mournful, watery look.

'S'ready,' yelled Maureen.

'What is it?' asked Tommy as he sat down at the kitchen table.

'What do you mean?'

'I mean, what is it?'

'It's stew, of course. Can't you tell?'

'Not really,' said Tommy.

'I don't like it,' cried Charlie. 'I want a jam butty.'

Tommy began to feel a little bit sorry for Maureen. He finished his dinner without further fuss. He slipped upstairs to see Mrs Mac but, as Maureen had said, she was asleep, so he returned to school.

Miss Bloom appeared to have spent the entire lunchtime 'doing' her eyes. They were green near her brows, blue in the middle, and black the rest of the way down. She looked like a beautiful witch. Normally, Tommy would have been interested, but this afternoon he felt very depressed. His mother rarely went to bed in the middle of the day. She often complained of headaches and 'nerves' but she rarely undressed and got into bed. He couldn't concentrate properly on the History lesson. It was something to do with Caesar deciding to conquer England, and fellows dashing around in some blue stuff called woad.

'Tommy!' called Miss Bloom.

'Who, miss? Me, miss?'

'Yes you, come out here.'

Tommy lumbered to the front of the class. Denise Davenport eyed him with venom.

'What's the matter with you, lad?' Miss Bloom wanted to know. 'You're staring out of the window like a fish with heart trouble.'

Tommy explained in a mumbling voice about his mother and stopped in horror as his voice began to crack.

'Oh, I see,' said Miss Bloom. 'Do you like humbugs?'

Tommy nodded.

'Well, finish this bag off for me. And read your library book.'

At home time, Miss Bloom intercepted Tommy at the school gate. She was sitting in a small blue car.

'Hop in,' she said. 'I think I'm going your way. I expect you want to get home to see how your mother is.'

To Tommy's delight, Mrs Mac was up and busily engaged in making lettuce and tomato sandwiches.

'May I come in?' called Miss Bloom.

Before Mrs Mac could say, 'Er, well . . .,' Miss Bloom was inside the house. Mrs Mac, who had supposed that she must be one of Maureen's friends, snatched off her pinny when Miss Bloom announced that she was, in fact, Tommy's new teacher.

'Would you like a cup of tea?' she asked.

'Thank you, I'd love one, that's very kind of you.' Miss Bloom sank down beside the sink and accepted the tea gratefully. It had been a rough day one way and another. 'Would you mind if I sent Tommy out for some humbugs?' she said. 'He ate all mine in the History lesson.'

Tommy sped off to the corner sweet shop, filled with relief. The sky was pink with evening light. Outside the sweet shop, Casey and Akim were slumped against the wall, chewing. They gave Tommy the usual terse greeting. Tommy paused and pretended to study the sweets displayed in the window. The aniseed balls had caught the sun and were fading badly. A large ginger cat lay dozing on top of the Spanish shoelaces.

'Got Miss Bloom to tea at our house,' boasted Tommy after a while.

'And yer Uncle Harry, too, I suppose,' mocked Casey.

'And the Queen in your front parlour, no doubt,' sniggered Akim.

'No. Just Miss Bloom.'

'Fall down a grid!' Casey jeered.

'All right then, hold on till I get these sweets and you can walk home with me. Then if you don't see her car outside our house you can have Nessy in your gang.'

'He's got a broken leg.'

'So what! It'll mend. He's coming out of hospital next week.'

Casey considered. Tommy sounded very sure of himself, but then he'd sounded very sure about his Uncle Harry and look how that had turned out. Tommy Mac was all talk and no brain. He'd pulled Casey's leg too often. This time Casey was going to be more cunning.

'A guy with a broken leg isn't much cop,' he said at last; 'I want yer transport, too.'

'Okay,' agreed Tommy lightheartedly.

Casey considered again. It was a tricky situation. 'I tell you what, I'll come after tea,' he said. 'I've just remembered we're having roast chicken; it'll be spoilt if I don't get in there at the beginning.'

He reckoned that if Tommy Mac was really telling the truth Miss Bloom might have left by the time he had finished his beans on toast, which is what the Caseys were really having for tea. Besides, there was a certain something about the expression on Tommy's face which rang true.

'If you go home first,' Tommy said, 'the deal's off. She's come for afternoon tea, not supper. Are you coming or aren't you? Of course,' he added slowly, 'if you think you *ought* to go home first for your chicken—I mean, if you think your mam might be annoyed . . .'

'We're coming,' Casey decided. It was obvious that Tommy was now trying to put them off.

Casey's rage knew no bounds when they arrived at Number Seven and found Miss Bloom's car parked outside. He could even hear her voice coming from inside the house.

'Teacher's pet!' he yelled furiously. 'Catch me having some old teacher in *our* house.'

'She's not old,' Tommy pointed out.

'Wait till the guys at school hear what a rotten little teacher's pet you are. Wait till . . .'

Tommy laughed in as irritating a manner as possible and then disappeared inside.

Miss Bloom was just coming out of the kitchen. She was laughing. They were all laughing. Charlie was laughing, and wondering why. Maureen was eyeing Miss Bloom's skirt enviously.

'My, she's a fine lass that,' said Mr Mac after Miss Bloom had left. 'Not much older than our Maureen but she's got her head screwed on the right way—and no side, either.'

Maureen looked sullen. 'S'all right for her,' she grumbled, 'she's got money.'

'Sure. She worked for it though. Ever think of working for anything, Maureen? That reminds me, you're all going to work a lot harder round here. Your poor mam slaves away for all of us. That's not fair.' Mr Mac looked solemnly at his offspring. 'Maureen,' he said, 'your job's beds. Mags and Kate, the washing up. Stevey, you'll bring up the coal; Tommy, the messages, and Charlie ...' Mr Mac picked up his youngest and placed him on his great knee. 'You just be a good boy, eh?'

The following Saturday, Nessy came out of hospital. He swaggered down the street, a crutch under his arm and his leg still in plaster. He had drawn skulls and weird monsters all over the cast. The gang flocked round him admiringly. His present disability was all the fault of Mrs McCann's cat, Chow Mein. It had become stuck on the 'chippy' roof—or so Nessy had thought—and he had gallantly climbed up to rescue it. But at the precise moment when he had been going to catch hold of it, Chow Mein had leapt gracefully to the ground, followed very shortly by Nessy and a couple of roof tiles.

'We've had a smashing time while you've been away,' Tommy was saying.

'Oh, thank you very much,' snorted Nessy. 'I'll do it again if you like.'

'No, I mean we've got a smashing new teacher,' Tommy explained.

'*No* teacher's smashing,' observed Nessy wisely.

'This one is!' chorused the gang indignantly.

'Never mind about teachers, I've just found a penny,' cried Nessy. He bent down to pick it up. 'D'you know,' he said thoughtfully, 'I bet people walk over pennies and things every day and never notice. I bet thousands of valuable things get washed down drains every day—well, more than you think anyway.'

'Let's start a finding club,' suggested Tommy, inspired by Nessy's enthusiasm. 'We'll split up for an hour then meet again and see what we've got.'

'Great,' said Nessy, sticking his plaster leg in the air.

'I'll take you on the go-cart,' Tommy grinned.

Later, they collected on Tommy's doorstep and emptied their pockets. Chai had found a watch face. It had no hands but was otherwise in a pretty good condition. Tommy and Nessy displayed a box of tacks and some rusty springs, and Chai had found a cigarette packet which actually contained one cigarette. They stared silently at their finds.

'Still, it just shows,' said Tommy; 'it does just show. I mean, we wouldn't even have found this if we'd just been walking round ordinarily.'

'And it did only take an hour,' Raff pointed out.

'Just it,' replied Tommy. 'Imagine what we could get if we looked all day.'

'Let's do it tomorrow,' suggested Raff.

The others readily agreed.

The following day was dull but warm—a good

sort of day for looking. Chai had optimistically brought a haversack with him. The gang arranged to hunt in pairs: Raff and Chai together, and Tommy with Nessy on the go-cart.

In the first five minutes, Nessy found a penny. He put it in his pocket for luck but it didn't seem to work for they found nothing else all that morning.

'Gosh, I'm famished,' sighed Tommy.

'Me too,' said Nessy. 'Shall we give up? It's pretty boring really.'

'But what if Raff and Chai beat us?'

'I'm too hungry to care,' moaned Nessy. He rubbed his stomach and rolled his eyes horribly.

Grudgingly, Tommy pulled him towards his home. It seemed a shame, he thought. They'd done so well the day before. He turned down an alley which led into Paradise Way. It was crowded with bins and he zig-zagged between them until Nessy yelled for mercy. Then Tommy stopped the go-cart with a jerk and picked something up.

'What is it?' asked Nessy.

'It's a book.'

'What sort?'

'I don't know but I've seen our Aunt Lil with one just like it.'

They sat down to examine it.

'Gosh, it says "Pension Book",' exclaimed Tommy excitedly. 'That's worth money.'

'What do you think we ought to do with it?' asked Nessy.

'It's got an address written on it. We'll have to take it back. Some poor old lady will be worrying herself to death about this.'

'I guess you're right,' agreed Nessy.

The address shown on the book was a place on the other side of the town. Tommy Mac helped Nessy on to a bus and they rode off in search of Mrs Hart-Smythe.

'Poor old lady,' Nessy kept repeating. 'She must be worried to death.'

The bus passed through the grey section of the town and into a more pleasant part. The conductor told them when to get off and a passer-by directed them to the address they wanted.

'Hope it's not far,' Nessy grumbled; 'this crutch is killing me.'

'It's not. We're here,' said Tommy.

An enormous house faced them. It was surrounded by beech and yew trees. A long gravel drive led up to a dazzling white front door. The two boys stared at it and hesitated.

'I don't think she *is* a poor old lady, you know,' said Tommy. 'Still, we'll have to give her the book back.'

'She might think we've pinched it!' said Nessy suddenly.

But Tommy had rung the bell. Perhaps Nessy was right, he thought. It might be less trouble to slip the pension book through the letter box. But at that moment the door was opened by a tall, severe woman. She eyed the two boys with suspicion and said icily, 'Yes?'

'Excuse me, missus,' stammered Tommy. 'I think this belongs to you.' He handed her the book and started down the drive.

'Wait a minute, boy,' commanded the tall

woman. 'I am not Mrs Hart-Smythe. You had better come inside while I fetch her. Sit there and don't touch anything.'

Tommy and Nessy entered the hall and sat nervously on the edge of a settee. Through an open door they could see a room crowded with statues and paintings. The lights looked like gold candles. There must have been at least a pound's worth of flowers in every vase, Tommy reckoned.

'I told you this wasn't a good idea,' whispered Nessy.

'No you didn't,' Tommy whispered back. 'You agreed.'

'Only till I saw the house, then I said stick the book in the letter box, but you'd gone and rung the bell. I bet you she's phoning the police right now.'

'Why should she? If we'd pinched her rotten book, we wouldn't be bringing it back, would we?'

'Ssh,' hissed Nessy, 'someone's coming.'

A small, plump woman entered the hall and bore down on the boys with outstretched hands.

'How *do* you do,' she cried, smiling broadly. 'My name is Mrs Hart-Smythe. I believe you boys found my pension book and brought it back to me?'

'Yes, missus,' said Tommy.

'I *do* think that's most awfully kind of you. I was visiting a friend in hospital last week and I must have dropped the book in a side street.'

'Yes, missus,' said Tommy again.

'And you've come *all* this way just to return it.'

'Me and my friend started a finding club so we just happened to be looking, that's all,' Tommy explained.

'I see. Well, you must have some tea before you go back. Come into the drawing room.'

The boys followed Mrs Hart-Smythe into the room filled with statues and paintings. She picked up a small bell and tinkled it daintily. As if by magic, a door opened and the tall woman swept in pushing a loaded tea trolley.

Mrs Hart-Smythe seemed to thoroughly enjoy the sight of the two boys eating. She pressed them to take yet another cake, and another, until even Tommy's iron constitution could stand no more. She wanted to know everything about them: the gang, their favourite lessons at school, how many brothers and sisters they had. Finally, she produced a purse and handed them a pound note each. Tommy and Nessy stared.

'Honesty must be rewarded,' beamed Mrs Hart-Smythe. 'Take it. I am delighted to have met two such nice boys.'

She showed them out and waved until they were out of sight.

'Gosh!' said Tommy on the bus home. 'Have you ever had so much money in your life?'

'Never,' said Nessy. 'Just think, we were going to give up!'

Raff and Chai had had a dismally unprofitable day. It was not until the following day that they learnt of Tommy and Nessy's good luck.

'I'm going to buy a transistor with my money,' declared Tommy. 'I've seen one in a second-hand shop and it's only a pound. I've always wanted a transistor and now I'm going to have one. You can all share it; I'll bring it out with me.'

They enjoyed school that day. Nessy immediately appreciated Miss Bloom. Mr Jones sauntered into the class and praised Tommy's progress, which made a very pleasant change. It was therefore a heavy blow when he returned home at tea time to find that his mother wasn't there. Mr Mac told him that she had gone down to the hospital.

'Is she going to die, or something?' Tommy asked anxiously.

'Heavens, no!' laughed Mr Mac; 'nothing like that. Your mam's a strong, healthy woman. But you could give her a surprise and tidy this room.'

Tommy had just finished when Mrs Mac arrived home. She looked hot and tired but there was a mysterious smile on her face.

'What did the hospital say?' asked Tommy breathlessly.

'Yes, what *did* they say, love?' asked Mr Mac.

Mrs Mac sat down at the table. She removed her hat, pin by pin. The suspense was agonising. Her behaviour was uncommonly secretive. She poured herself a cup of tea and took a long, long drink.

Then she said, 'I'm going to have twins.'

'Twins!' shouted Mr Mac; 'twins—oh Mam!' He put his arms around her like a great bear, and rocked her to and fro.

'Twins!' echoed Tommy weakly.

In the hubbub that followed, Tommy slipped out and ran to a florist's shop.

'I want a quid's worth of flowers,' he panted; 'the very best you've got.' He produced the pound note as he saw the hesitation in the florist's face.

'Are they for your mother?' the woman asked.

'Yes,' said Tommy proudly. 'She's going to have twins.'

'My goodness!' laughed the woman. '*That* doesn't happen every day.' She persuaded Tommy to buy a plant instead of cut flowers. 'It will last much longer,' she assured him. 'Here's one in bud. I know your mother will be pleased with that.'

Mrs Mac was. She stared speechlessly at the magnificent plant and she drew Tommy tightly to her. She didn't say thank you; she just hugged him and said, over and over again, 'Oh! Our Tommy!'

Tommy Mac sat on the doorstep of Number Seven, Paradise Way. It was beginning to rain. He could hear the ships' sirens on the river. Dracula and Count were barking in the yard, answering the dogs in the street. Mags and Kate were squabbling, as usual, and Maureen and Stevey were watching television. It was singularly peaceful.

Tommy Mac understood why his mother hadn't said thank you; Mrs Hart-Smythe would have said it a hundred times but Tommy understood his mam—having twins was the best thank you she could have given him. He would take them for rides on his go-cart and teach them to fight Casey. He would show them how to get into school late without being caught by Mr Jones and how to climb, and how to ride donkeys. He might even teach them to act. There was no end to the things Tommy Mac could teach the twins, and he could hardly wait.